✦ G R E A T ✦
IMPOSTERS

GEORGE SULLIVAN

SCHOLASTIC INC.
New York Toronto London Auckland Sydney

ISBN 0-590-48714-0

12 11 10 9 8 7 6 5 4 3 2 1   11   4 5 6 7 8 9/9

Printed in the U.S.A.   01

Contents

Introduction

An impostor, says the dictionary, is a person who practices deception under an assumed name or character.

The stories in this book concern impostors of every type, from the sixteen-year-old high school dropout who successfully masqueraded as an airline pilot, to the Brooklyn file clerk who managed to arrange a White House reception for himself and a guest; from the English chambermaid who escaped a life of servitude by posing as a sister to the queen, to the bogus French count who twice sold the Eiffel Tower to gullible scrap-iron dealers.

Why does one become an impostor? There are several reasons. Some do it for the excitement and thrills that come from exhibiting oneself in another's identity. Others do it for the recognition and fame they're able to achieve. For others, money is the sole motive.

But all impostors have one thing in common. They live by their wits. There is no limit to their cleverness, ingenuity, and boldness. They are a special breed of people.

Chapter 1

Willie the Actor

Among the great thieves of history, Willie Sutton was one of a kind. In executing a robbery, Willie would dress up in a uniform, working clothes, or a business suit, using his disguise to slip by a guard or gain entry to a building. His nickname, "Willie the Actor," suited him to perfection.

During a career of crime that covered almost half a century, Willie used dozens of different disguises. He was a mailman, window cleaner, fireman, police officer, chauffeur, and Western Union messenger.

He was so convincing in the various roles he played that it was often said he might have been a successful actor if he had pursued that profession. But Willie much preferred stealing for a living. It was more challenging, he believed, and he got great satisfaction from his successes. It was also, on occasion, quite profitable.

A disguise was only one aspect of the careful

planning that went into every one of Willie's productions. He would study his target for days, even weeks. He would get to know the habits of the employees, the routines followed by the guards and the local police who patrolled the streets. He would draw up a floor plan of a jewelry store or a bank, showing the various exits, entrances, and alarm locations.

But Willie the Actor was also Willie the Loser. He spent thirty-three of his seventy-nine years behind bars. When he died, he did not have a penny of the more than two million dollars he claimed to have stolen.

Willie was brought up in a tough Irish neighborhood in Brooklyn, New York. His life of crime began at a very early age. When he was only nine, he broke into a grocery store and robbed the cash register of six dollars in change.

He and his young friends stole fruit and vegetables, candy, and tobacco. Willie's parents were churchgoing, law-abiding people who found it hard to believe that their son, not yet ten years old, had earned a reputation as a thief.

As a teenager, Willie spent most of his time in a local poolroom. There he met a safecracker of long experience, Doc Tate. The older man took a liking to Willie and invited him to take part in a jewelry store holdup in Wilkes Barre, Pennsylvania. The job netted the two men about sixty thousand dollars.

Over the next three years, Doc Tate and Willie planned and executed many robberies. Willie was learning a trade.

He also began learning how to enjoy himself.

He lived in fine hotels and dined on the best food. He dressed stylishly and spent his evenings at night clubs and the Broadway theater.

Willie and Doc broke up in 1925, and for several years Willie was on his own. In 1930, he went to work for Dutch Schultz, a mob leader of the time. But Schultz used Willie merely as a collection agent and a messenger.

Willie decided he would strike out on his own again, using the skills he had learned from Doc Tate. In 1934, Willie used an acetylene torch in an attempt to crack the vault of a bank in Long Island, New York. But the alarm sounded before he could complete the job. Willie was caught and sent to prison.

Behind bars, he had plenty of time to think. He realized that by using an acetylene torch he had established a particular way of operating for himself, what the police call a *modus operandi*, or M.O. If, after his release, he used an acetylene torch again and escaped, police records would be consulted. His name would be listed among those who used acetylene torches in the past. Sutton made up his mind to change his M.O., to find a new method of operation.

One evening in the spring of 1939, not long after he had been released from prison, Sutton was walking along New York's Fifth Avenue, when he saw an armored car stop in front of a tall office building. It was just after six o'clock and the door of the building was locked. Two uniformed armed guards got out of the truck and went to the locked door of the building. One of them pressed the bell. Almost immediately a guard appeared and unlocked the door, admitting the two men.

The scene fascinated Sutton. The fact that two men could gain entry to a locked building so quickly and easily started his mind working.

What did it was the uniform, Sutton thought to himself. The building security guard had probably never seen the two guards from the armored truck before. By wearing the right uniform, in the right place, at the right time, it might be possible to gain entry to almost any building — a department store, jewelry store, or bank. "Willie the Actor" was about to launch his career.

Willie began by getting in touch with a former partner in crime, Jack Barton. The two men rented a small office, telling the landlord they planned to open a school for actors. It was to be called the Oxford Dramatic School. They even had stationery and business cards printed.

The next step was to send letters to several companies that specialized in renting costumes for theatrical productions. Each letter announced that the Oxford Dramatic School was staging several different productions. For one of these, a Western Union messenger's uniform was needed.

Within a few days, Willie began receiving replies. Send the actor to us, one letter said, and we will fit him with a uniform.

It was Sutton himself who went to the costume company for the fitting. When he walked into the showroom, his heart pounded at what he saw. There were uniforms of every description hanging from pipe racks. Sutton could become a priest, a letter carrier, a naval officer, an airline pilot, a judge, fireman, or policeman. And the uniforms looked so genuine that no one would ever suspect that they were meant for the stage.

A salesman came forward to help. Willie introduced himself as an actor and showed the salesman the letter from the costume company to the Oxford Dramatic School. "Do you have a messenger's uniform in my size?" he asked.

"I'm sure we do," the salesman said. "We have all sizes."

Before long, Willie was standing before a full-length mirror, admiring the trim, olive green uniform with polished brass buttons. Just perfect, he thought to himself.

Willie and Jack Barton had picked out a bank in the borough of Queens as their target. It was located in a quiet neighborhood with only a few stores nearby.

By watching the bank carefully for several days, Willie familiarized himself with the employees' routines. The first employee, a uniformed guard, arrived shortly before eight o'clock. Once he admitted himself, he stood behind the locked entrance door, opening it to other employees who showed their identification cards. By eight-thirty, all but one or two of the seven employees had arrived. At nine o'clock, the bank opened for business.

Only one piece of the puzzle was missing. Sutton needed a telegram. He visited a Western Union office and arranged to send a telegram to his own company, the Oxford Dramatic School. When it arrived, he steamed the envelope open and threw the message away. On a sheet of yellow paper, he typed the bank manager's name and the address of the bank, then inserted the paper in the Western Union envelope so that the name and address showed through the envelope's glassine window.

Early the next morning, Willie donned the messenger's uniform and tucked the fake telegram into his pocket. Jack Barton drove him to Queens and dropped him a few blocks from the bank.

At precisely two minutes past eight o'clock, Willie appeared at the bank's entrance. He rang the bell. When the guard came to the door, Willie held up the telegram so the guard could see the name and address. "Telegram for the boss," he said.

The guard unlocked the door and opened it a crack, motioning Willie to slip the telegram through. "You've got to sign for it," Willie said, and produced a notebook and a pen.

The guard swung the door open. Willie handed him the notebook and the pen. As the guard started to sign, writing with his right hand and supporting the notebook with his left, Willie reached down and plucked the guard's pistol from its holster.

The guard gasped. "W-what's going on?" he said.

Willie grinned. "Now just behave yourself and nothing will happen," he said. The guard raised his hands over his head. "Just step back away from the door," Willie told him.

At that moment, as planned, Jack Barton arrived. He took up a position by the front door.

Willie and Jack knew that the other employees

would start arriving any minute. Willie moved behind a counter, keeping the pistol pointed at the guard. "When the other people start arriving, open the door and let each one in," Willie ordered. "Don't try anything funny. I don't want to hurt you, so don't force me to."

The guard nodded.

The next half hour passed swiftly and without a hitch. The employees began arriving. The guard, although trembling, admitted them one by one. Each employee was ordered to sit down. Jack Barton watched over them, gun in hand.

The last person to arrive was the bank manager. Willie persuaded him to open the vault. "Why risk lives for the sake of money?" he asked him.

Inside the vault, there were several metal boxes containing about a quarter of a million dollars in new bills. While Jack guarded the employees, Willie stuffed the money into a cloth sack.

As the two men were leaving, Willie ordered the employees to stay in their seats for at least ten more minutes. "We have a third associate outside," he said. "If anyone should decide to run outside, or run anywhere to use a telephone, our man may be forced to use his gun." Then Willie and Jack backed out of the bank, turned, and walked hurriedly to their car. Later that day, they laughed heartily as they divided their money and recounted all that happened in the bank.

But Willie was not always so successful. Several times his careful plans went awry, and he ended up in the hands of the law. One of his miscalculations earned him a long sentence in the Eastern State Penitentiary. After twelve years of confinement, he managed to escape.

He headed for New York City. Once settled there, he resumed his career as an impostor.

On one occasion, he played the role of a New York fire inspector, wearing an inspector's dark blue uniform and white peaked hat. He called upon a well-known Fifth Avenue jeweler and told him that his store required an inspection.

"Go right ahead," said the jeweler. "Do whatever you have to do." Willie had to fight hard to hold back a smile.

"I think I'll start with the back room," Willie said.

"Fine," said the jeweler, and he led Willie toward the back of the store.

Once they were alone in the back room, Willie cracked the jeweler on the head. Then he scooped up sixty thousand dollars in expensive gems and made his escape before the jeweler regained consciousness. Although the jeweler identified him from photographs, Willie could not be tracked down. It was as if he had vanished.

Willie was at it again in 1950. He masterminded the holdup of another bank in Queens, getting away with sixty-four thousand dollars. By putting together all available evidence, police deduced that it was Willie who had performed the job.

The Federal Bureau of Investigation distributed handbills bearing Willie's photographs to department stores, banks, and post offices throughout the country, with the recommendation that they be posted. Willie's face became known to tens of thousands of people.

One of the handbills reached a clothing store in Brooklyn, New York, operated by Max Schuster.

8

His son, Arnold, who worked in the store, paid little attention to it. But his father tacked up the handbill above the desk in the store's office. Day after day, young Arnold saw the picture.

One morning in February, 1952, Arnold boarded a subway for downtown Brooklyn where the clothing store was located. When he noticed a slim, neatly dressed man seated across the aisle from him, Arnold's heart skipped a beat. It was Willie Sutton! Arnold was sure of it.

When the train stopped at the Pacific Street Station, and the man got up to leave, Arnold followed him. Out on the street, Arnold spotted a police car. He ran up to it and told the two officers he was shadowing Willie Sutton.

Sutton was seated in a parked car when Arnold and the two policemen approached him. He heatedly denied that he was Willie Sutton. Arnold was sure he had made a mistake. But the cops didn't believe him. One watched Willie while the other called for help.

Later that year, Sutton went on trial, was found guilty, and sentenced to from thirty years to life for the Queens bank robbery. He served seventeen years before he was paroled in 1969. He was white-haired, in poor health, and nearly seventy years of age.

Two months after his release, Willie appeared at a welfare office in Brooklyn. He said he needed seventy dollars for food and rent until he received money for a book he was writing. The book, titled *Where the Money Was,* was published in 1976.

Later, Willie moved to Florida where he lived with his sister. He died in 1980.

"I prefer to think of myself as an artist, a

showman, rather than a thief," he once declared. "I never hurt anyone. I rarely carried a gun. I didn't like to use a gun. If I did, it was only to threaten someone. I don't think I could ever shoot anyone. My greatest feeling of satisfaction came when I could hoax someone into believing I was something other than myself . . . and make a profit out of it."

Chapter 2

Bad Habit

Newsweek magazine once called him "The Persistent Phony." To *Time*, he was a "Superior Sort of Liar." When Robert Crichton wrote his biography in the late 1950s, he labeled him "The Great Impostor."

His real name was Ferdinand Waldo Demara, Jr. Over a period that began in the early 1940s and covered almost two decades, Demara, a high school dropout, assumed several professional roles before settling down as an ordained minister of the Gospel.

The chubby, crew-cut Demara posed as a Trappist monk in a Kentucky monastery, a professor of psychology at a Pennsylvania college, a biologist specializing in cancer research, and the recreational officer of a maximum security prison.

Demara's greatest feat occurred during the Korean War when he served as a doctor in the Canadian Navy. Thanks to some previous training and the aid of medical books, Demara pulled teeth, removed tonsils, amputated limbs, and once successfully removed a bullet lodged near the heart of a badly wounded Korean soldier.

Except for a few months he once spent in a civilian jail, and the one-and-one-half years he spent in a military prison for deserting from the Navy during World War II, Demara was seldom punished for his hoaxes.

Demara was once asked why he felt compelled to spend most of his adult life fooling people. He replied, "Being an impostor is a tough habit to break."

Ferdinand Demara, whom everyone would call Fred, was born on December 12, 1921, in Lawrence, Massachusetts. His father owned several successful movie theaters and the family lived in an elegant house on Jackson Street in the wealthy section of the city. They had several servants.

Young Fred was bigger and stronger than most of the children his age. Other boys and girls usually left him alone. Fred didn't mind that; he could entertain himself for hours at a time. When he did play with other children, he always wanted to be the leader. If he couldn't lead, he wouldn't play.

When Fred was twelve years old, his father lost his money. The family had to move out of the big house into crowded quarters in a poor neighborhood. Fred had to wear heavy and stiff black boots and corduroy knickers. He hated being poor. He dreamed of the day when the family would return to the house on Jackson Street, but that day never came.

When Fred went to high school, he tried out for the football team and won a position on the squad. But he didn't like the game's violence or the discipline. He gave up the idea of becoming a football player.

He was never able to get used to the shabby surroundings of his home. He knew he couldn't stay with his family, even though he loved them.

One day he left for school but never reached his destination. Instead, he sold his bicycle to get enough money to buy a train ticket to Providence, Rhode Island. From there he took a bus to the nearby town of Valley Falls.

Fred had once heard that a monastery at Valley Falls, which was operated by the Trappist monks, never turned away anyone who knocked at its door. Fred appeared at the monastery and asked to be admitted — and was.

For a Trappist monk, the day begins at two o'clock in the morning with the worship of God. A breakfast of hard bread and a hot drink is served at five-thirty. Hard, physical labor begins after breakfast and lasts until eleven-thirty. At the main meal of the day, each monk receives a small bowl of soup, two vegetables, bread, and fruit. The afternoon is devoted to more hard, physical work, and then a scanty evening meal is served.

The most difficult part of life at Valley Fields was that absolute silence had to be observed for the entire day. Speaking was only permitted if it was necessary to carry out one's assigned duties. Although Fred was not considered a monk, he was made to follow this way of life.

Fred was put in charge of two stubborn mules and assigned to plow the fields. He spent most of the day shouting at the mules, named Lucifer and Luther. "Come on there, Lucifer," he would say. "Gee boy, gee. Let go there, Luther." In the evening, when the other monks were yearning to speak, Fred would be too hoarse to talk.

Fred learned to sidestep one rule after another. Once each day, the monks were allowed to take an extra amount of bread, if it was considered essential. Fred never failed to take the added portions, sometimes helping himself to five or six pieces.

One day, as a joke, a fellow monk put a three-foot-long loaf of bread at Fred's place at the table. The monk thought this might embarrass Fred, but it didn't. Using sign language, he said, "What? Only one piece of bread with my soup?"

His parents and those who knew Fred doubted he would remain in the monastery for more than a few weeks. He stayed two years. When the abbot and others in charge told him they did not believe he was cut out for monastery life, Fred was deeply hurt.

Fred returned home, but stayed only a short time. He joined another religious order, the Brothers of Charity, but when he felt his talents as a teacher were not appreciated, he picked up and left.

Then he joined the United States Army. He quickly found Army life impossible. One day he walked off the base where he was stationed and never went back.

Using the name of an Army friend, he joined an order of Trappist monks in Kentucky. Unfortunately, someone recognized him there as Fred Demara, and he was forced to skip town.

Not long after the outbreak of World War II, Demara joined the Navy. He didn't like being a sailor any more than a soldier. He deserted.

Assuming the fictitious identity of one Robert Linton French, Demara, posing as a college professor, drifted from one Midwestern college to another, usually remaining until his real identity was discovered and he was asked to leave. But at Erie College in Gannon, Pennsylvania, he became the Dean of the School of Psychology and enjoyed an extended stay.

One day in September, 1950, Demara set out for a school operated by the Brothers of Christian Instruction in the town of Alfred, Maine. They quickly offered him a teaching position.

During this period, Demara met Dr. Joseph Cyr, a Canadian doctor. They became good friends. One day, Dr. Cyr asked Demara whether he might help him get a license that would enable him to pursue his profession in the United States.

"I'll do what I can," said Demara. "Give me copies of all your records and credentials."

After a few days, the unsuspecting Dr. Cyr brought Demara a stack of papers several inches high. At the time, Demara probably had no intention of using the papers for his own purposes. But the following year, when Demara's scheme involving the Brothers of Christian Instruction went awry, the thought occurred to him that he still had Dr. Cyr's credentials in his possession.

So it was then that Demara appeared at a Royal Canadian Navy recruiting office in St. John, New Brunswick, in March 1951, announcing himself as Dr. Joseph Cyr, and inquiring whether he could volunteer his services.

This was the time of the Korean War, and the Canadian Navy had a fierce need for doctors. Navy officials were overjoyed that Dr. Cyr wanted

15

to enlist. He was placed aboard a Navy plane and flown to Ottawa. There he was interviewed and his papers were hurriedly checked. Soon after, he was commissioned a surgeon general in the Royal Canadian Navy and assigned to duty at the big Canadian naval base at Halifax, Nova Scotia.

Upon arrival at the base, Demara was in charge of sick call, a daily formation of those who required medical attention. Most of the patients he treated suffered only from minor ills, coughs, and sore throats or the like. Demara always prescribed penicillin for such ailments.

When he was confronted by someone who stayed sick or seemed seriously ill, Demara would prevail upon one of the six or seven real doctors at the base to examine the patient. "What do you think of this case?" he would ask. The doctor, after examining the patient, would give his opinion. Demara never failed to make use of it.

After several weeks of duty at the naval base, Demara was transferred for a short stay to the giant aircraft carrier *Magnificent*, which was anchored in Halifax Bay. He then received orders to report to the *Cayuga*, a destroyer, as the ship's medical officer.

The *Cayuga*, manned by eight officers and two hundred and eleven seamen, was not a big ship. It was assigned to combat duty in the Pacific Ocean.

Demara's status was much different aboard the *Cayuga* than it had been at the naval base in Halifax or during his tour of duty on the *Magnificent*. Always before, there were other doctors with whom he could consult. But on the *Cayuga* he was on his own. The lives of any one of more than two hundred men could depend on him at

16

any time. This thought troubled Demara as the *Cayuga* sailed westward across the Pacific.

Demara's first crisis was not long in coming. He was told the ship's captain was sick and was summoned to his cabin.

As soon as he saw the captain, he knew what was wrong. His jaw was so swollen he looked as if he was holding a plum in one cheek. He had several infected teeth.

"Pull these damn things!" the captain declared. "That's an order!"

Demara peered into the captain's mouth. "Have them out in a jiffy," he said. "But I have to go down to my cabin and get my equipment."

As he hurried to his cabin, it occurred to Demara that he didn't know how to pull a tooth. He wasn't even sure what instrument to use.

When he reached his cabin, he started going through his medical books, seeking information on how to pull a tooth. There was nothing.

Then he heard someone pounding on his door. "Dr. Cyr! Dr. Cyr! The captain says to please hurry."

"I'm getting my medical gear together," Demara replied. "I'll be another minute or two."

Demara continued to leaf through the pages of his medical books, desperate for information. Fifteen minutes went by.

Someone was pounding on the door again. "Dr. Cyr! Is everything all right? The captain *orders* you to come immediately."

Demara knew he could wait no longer. He put the equipment he needed into a small black bag and returned to the captain's cabin.

He began by injecting novocaine into the captain's jaw. After a few moments, he tapped the captain's cheek. "Feel anything?" he asked.

The captain shook his head from side to side.

Demara took a pair of forceps, found the bad tooth, clamped on to it, and began pulling. It came out so easily that Demara momentarily lost his balance and almost fell backward. The second tooth came out as easily as the first.

Demara went back to his room and put away his equipment. He heard nothing until the next morning when he was strolling the deck and caught sight of the captain. He rushed up to Demara and shook his hand.

"Nicest job of tooth pulling I've ever had," the captain said. "Glad to have you aboard this ship, Cyr."

Demara grinned. He felt very pleased with himself.

The *Cayuga* made its way westward, stopping off in Japan for repairs, then heading south, into waters off the east coast of Korea. The ship's assignment was to observe North Korean shore operations. From time to time, the *Cayuga*'s guns would be trained on enemy fortifications or troop emplacements and blast away for several hours.

It was a period of calm for Demara. One day a seaman picked up a red-hot shell casing and burned his hands. But that was the worst problem that Demara had to face.

Deep inside, Demara had a feeling that things were not going to stay peaceful indefinitely. One day he was going to be severely tested.

It happened even sooner than he expected. One afternoon late in September, with the sea rough and choppy, one of the lookouts aboard the *Cayuga* spotted a small Korean junk. Men aboard the boat were trying to establish contact with the *Cayuga*. Officers aboard the *Cayuga* felt it might be a trick of some kind. With the help of a Korean officer based on board, they signaled the junk to cut its engines and drop anchor.

Slowly the *Cayuga* pulled up alongside the junk. When the men of the *Cayuga* looked down into the junk, what they saw sickened them. On the deck, sprawled in their own blood, lay the mutilated bodies of more than a dozen Korean soldiers.

"They were caught in an ambush," the Korean officer explained. "They want to know whether there's someone on board who can help them."

"My God," one sailor said. "They need help. Get Dr. Cyr!"

Others echoed what the first man had said. "Get Dr. Cyr!"

When Demara was brought to the scene and he looked down into the junk, he knew he had to help. If the men were left untreated on the deck of the junk, some of them were certain to die. "I'm going down there," he announced to the captain.

He climbed over the side and clambered down a rope ladder. He was startled by how young the soldiers were. Many of them were boys. He ordered that they be removed from the junk and brought aboard the *Cayuga* for treatment.

There were nineteen wounded soldiers in all. Once Demara had a chance to examine them and learn the extent of their injuries, he established that sixteen had wounds that were not serious.

But three of the men had suffered grave injuries. If they did not receive surgery, it is likely that they would die.

For several hours, Demara worked on the sixteen soldiers who were less seriously injured. He cleaned and stitched their wounds, then bandaged them.

He feared treating the other three men. One mistake, he knew, and he could take a life. But he felt he had no choice but to attempt to do whatever he could.

The room he had been using was too small for major surgery. He had to take over the captain's cabin, first having ordering it to be scrubbed with disinfectant.

The first soldier brought to him had been shot by a large-caliber bullet. It had shattered bone and ripped into his internal organs. Demara knew that if the man was to live he would have to stop the internal bleeding and perhaps remove the bullet, if it was still lodged inside him.

Once the patient was under anesthesia, Demara, using the sharp blade of his scalpel, made an incision in his chest under the jagged hole left by the bullet, clamping off the blood vessels as he cut them. With a rib spreader, he made an opening between two ribs. He could now see the fibrous covering in which the heart and blood vessels leading from it were contained.

Near the heart, he saw a tender-looking area where bleeding was occurring. He drew out the blood with a hypodermic syringe. He then could see part of the bullet. He reached in with a forceps, got a firm grip on it, and pulled. The bullet slid out fairly easily.

The next step was to clot the blood with a special foam. The rest was not difficult. He closed the wound with stitches, bandaged it, and ordered the patient to be taken away.

The next two soldiers were not as bad as the first. One had a wound on the inside of the thigh. The other had a chest wound which needed treatment for infection. When he finished with the last two patients, Demara was amazed to see that it was light outside. He had worked through the night.

Demara went to his room and slept for almost twenty-four hours. When he awakened, he went to check on his patients. They were gone.

"Where are the Koreans?" he asked one of his assistants. "Where are my patients?"

"Oh, they all got up and climbed down into the junk during the night. They wanted to go to Chinnampo." Chinnampo, Demara knew, was the heavily bombed island of mud huts where the Koreans lived.

Not long after Demara's heroic efforts aboard the *Cayuga*, the ship was sent back to Japan for repairs. While it was there, a Royal Navy information officer visited the vessel. When he learned of Dr. Cyr's exploits, he knew he was on to a good story. Later, when the *Cayuga* returned to Korean waters, and Demara had an opportunity to visit Chinnampo and examine and treat his patients, the information officer kept track of what was going on.

Calling Demara the Royal Canadian Navy's "miracle doctor," he released a story about him to newspapers throughout Canada. The story was to prove Demara's undoing. Not long after its release, the telephone started ringing in the home of Dr. Joseph Cyr in the Canadian town of Edmonton. And it kept ringing. The callers wanted to know if he was the Dr. Joseph Cyr who had been in Korea.

At first, Dr. Cyr thought the mix-up was based on a coincidence. "There are lots of Joseph Cyrs in the world," he told those who called. Then the local newspaper printed a picture of the Korean miracle doctor. Dr. Cyr was stunned by the picture, recognizing the man as a friend from the days he had spent with the Brothers of Christian Instruction.

The newspaper in Dr. Cyr's hometown was the first to reveal the truth. Then a paper in Toronto picked up the story. Eventually, Navy officials in Ottawa learned of the case. They quickly came to the conclusion that the Dr. Joseph Cyr aboard the *Cayuga* was an impostor. A message was sent to the *Cayuga* ordering that Dr. Cyr be suspended from duty immediately.

When the captain received the message, he thought it was a foolish mistake. "Don't worry about it," he told Demara. "We'll get it straightened out."

But that night, when he realized that this chapter in his life was about to end, Demara began to weep and became hysterical. He was flown back to Canada in the company of a medical officer and a security guard.

A board of inquiry was called into session. Demara admitted that he had entered the Navy under false pretenses and that his name was not Joseph Cyr. But he never stopped claiming he was a real doctor.

The Royal Canadian Navy never disputed his claim. Perhaps they realized that further investigation would only lead to further embarrassment. On November 21, 1951, they simply discharged him.

Demara returned to his parents' home in Lawrence, Massachusetts. He found that he was now a nationally known celebrity. Newspapers and magazines clamored for interviews.

He took a job with the Institute of Child Guidance in Massachusetts as an instructor named Fred Demara. But he didn't stay there very long. Over the next year or so, he drifted to Pittsburgh and Kansas City and also worked for a state school for the mentally retarded in upstate New York.

Texas came next. In Houston one day, he read that the Department of Correction of the State of Texas had several jobs open. He made application and was invited to interview at the Huntsville, Texas, prison, the largest in the South. He was asked to provide letters from previous employers and other individuals who would recommend him for the job. This he managed to do by one means of fakery or another.

He was hired as a lieutenant-of-the-guard at Huntsville. B.W. Jones was the name he had taken for himself. But everyone called him B.W.

Officials of the correction system in Texas believed that prisons were meant to punish people, not reform them. Violence and force were common. But Demara believed that the prison population was made up of sick children, for the most part, who needed love and understanding.

Prison authorities allowed him to set up

checkers and domino tournaments, and he was successful in getting a Ping-Pong table. He organized letter-writing sessions.

Given enough time, Demara probably would have made significant changes in the Texas prison system. But one day one of the inmates happened to read a magazine article about "The Great Impostor," Fred Demara. "Hey, what's B.W. Jones doing in this magazine?" the prisoner wanted to know.

The script then followed a familiar pattern. When authorities learned of the article, Demara fled. He was arrested in Florida, but Texas officials didn't press charges. It would have been too great an embarrassment for them. This, too, was becoming part of the pattern.

After two other stopovers, Demara landed at North Haven, an island-bound school in Maine's Penobscot Bay. There he taught Latin, using the name Martin Godgart.

When this hoax was discovered, Demara was arrested, brought to trial, and found guilty. But the state of Maine set him free. Once again, Demara returned to Massachusetts.

Why did Demara do it? Why did he spend his entire adult life seeking to be someone he wasn't?

That's a question for a psychiatrist to answer. But there can be no denying that certain events in his boyhood were highly significant. When Demara's father lost his money and his standing in the community, and the family was turned out of their luxurious home, young Demara was deeply hurt.

He lost his social status, for one thing. It's been said that he went through life trying to reclaim that status by assuming the identity of individuals who held positions of respect.

There were other theories, of course. One was put forth by a man who knew Demara at North Haven. He said, "You know, all of the time he was out here I always had the feeling he was laughing at us. Not hard, you know, or nasty, but laughing like he was enjoying a great big secret all his own. He had a real lot of fun posing."

Chapter 3

Princess of Pretense

High society has always been a favorite target of impostors. An individual not born into a circle of wealth or prominence will simply begin acting as if he or she were. It's been going on for centuries.

In earlier times, clever impostors would concentrate their energies on the kings and queens of Europe and the many people who attended them. There is, for example, the case of Sarah Wilson, born in the English village of Staffordshire in the year 1755. Her father worked as the overseer of a large estate, a position of great responsibility but poor wages.

When Sarah was sixteen, she was sent off to London to find a job as a maid in one of the many wealthy households of the day. Sarah was dark-haired, bright-eyed, and quick-witted, and so it was not altogether by chance that she was able to find a position as a chambermaid to Caroline Vernon, one of the attendants of the German-born Queen Charlotte, wife of King George III.

Thus, while still in her teens, Sarah found herself living in the royal palace (located on the site of the present Buckingham Palace), amidst great riches, exquisite clothes, and enormous power.

Although she did not serve Queen Charlotte directly, Sarah saw much of her. She began to develop a deep-seated envy of the Queen and of all the people who attended her. They enjoyed a life that Sarah could only dream of, and yet they were no better than she was, and many lacked her charm and intelligence. Sarah began to feel as if these people owed her something.

One day when the royal family was away, Sarah, acting on the spur of the moment, went into a small room off the Queen's bedchamber where her clothing and jewelry were stored. She rummaged through the drawers of a dressing table, picking out several items of jewelry that appealed to her — a pair of gold earrings, an emerald ring, an ornate brooch, a necklace of semiprecious stones, and a small portrait of the Queen herself. Before leaving, she also helped herself to two of the Queen's dresses.

The Queen owned such an enormous array of clothing and jewelry that Sarah believed the theft might never be discovered. But she was wrong. Queen Charlotte soon noticed that some of her most valuable pieces of jewelry were missing and instructed guards to keep a close watch on the room where the suspected theft had occurred.

Her first foray had been so successful it was inevitable that Sarah would return for a second helping of the Queen's valuables. When she did, she was caught red-handed.

In those days, the penalty for both violating the

royal privacy and theft was death. But Caroline Vernon took pity on Sarah and asked the Queen to show mercy on her behalf. After all, she was only seventeen. The Queen agreed to commute Sarah's sentence, ordering, instead, that she be deported to the English colonies in America. In July, 1771, Sarah was put aboard a prison ship bound for Baltimore in the colonial Palantinate, or Province, of Maryland.

Upon arrival in the colonies, Sarah, along with the other prisoners, was put on the auction block. The winning bid for her was posted by William Devall, a Maryland planter of Bush Creek, Frederick County. After a brief stay at the Devall household, where she served as a kitchen maid, Sarah packed her belongings and escaped to Virginia.

When she had left England, Sarah had been canny enough to bring with her the Queen's dresses, jewelry, and the portrait of the Queen. Using these items, Sarah cast herself in the new role, that of Princess Susanna Caroline Matilda, the sister of Queen Charlotte. She concocted a story that Princess Susanna had quarreled with the royal family and had been banished to the colonies because of a developing scandal. Not only was Sarah able to dress appropriately for the part she was playing, she spoke and behaved in a royal manner, having carefully observed members of the court during the time she had spent at the palace.

Sarah was an overnight success in her masquerade. Robert Smyth, a wealthy Virginia landowner, invited Sarah to stay with his family. At parties at the Smyth mansion, Sarah was the center of attraction, entertaining guests with court gossip and accounts of scandals involving the best-known people of London. Most of the settlers longed for news from England, and Sarah's colorful tales caused them to listen in open-mouthed wonderment.

Before long, the wealthiest families of Virginia were vying for the honor of entertaining the Princess. "She travels from one house to another," said a newspaper account of her doings, "and makes astonishing impressions in many places, affecting the mode of royalty with such perfection that many have the honor to kiss her hand." After a stay of several weeks with the Smyth family, Sarah journeyed to North Carolina and South Carolina, always living with the richest families.

Little by little, Sarah embellished her role, hinting that despite her disagreement with the royal family, she still had influence at the palace. She would listen attentively to those who sought royal favors, promising that she would do what she could on each petitioner's behalf. She had not the slightest reluctance to accept money and gifts in return for the assistance she promised.

If there were any suspicions that the Princess was as fictional as Snow White, no one voiced them. And there was much in her fabrication that could have been open to question. Just the statement that she was the younger sister of the Queen should have raised some eyebrows. It was generally known that the Queen had an older sister who lived in Germany. But a younger one? Anybody who had bothered to take a close look would have quickly recognized the person of the Princess had been hurriedly grafted to the Queen's family tree.

Someone might also have questioned the Princess's quite excellent English, surprisingly good for an individual who had been born and brought up in Germany. Occasionally someone would address her in German. Sarah would scowl and refuse to answer. "I'm an *English* princess," she would say. "And English is what I speak."

Tales of Sarah and her adventures began to work their way back to William Devall who immediately launched a campaign to get her back. Devall had hundreds of handbills printed which were distributed in the Southern cities and towns where Sarah had been seen. The handbills read as follows:

> Run away from her subscriber, a servant maid, named Sarah Wilson, but who changed her name to Lady Susanna Caroline Matilda, which made the public believe that she was Her Majesty's sister. She has a blemish in her right eye, black rolled hair, stoops in her shoulders, and makes a common practice of marking all of her clothing with a crown. Whoever secures said servant woman, or takes her home, shall receive five pistols, besides all costs and charges.

Devall assigned Michael Dalton, an employee of his, to track down Sarah. Dalton followed Sarah's trail to Charleston, South Carolina, where she was living on a plantation on the outskirts of the city. Dalton marched Sarah back to Devall at the point of his pistol.

For the next two years, Sarah performed her

daily chores in the Devall household. If she was unhappy, she gave little hint of it.

Nevertheless, Sarah was constantly looking for a chance to escape again. The chance came in 1776. England and her American colonies had grown apart. When the English sought to assert an increasing amount of control over colonial affairs, the colonists rebelled. Fighting began near Boston in April, 1775. The colonies declared their independence on July 4, 1776. George Washington took up the task of organizing the American forces. William Devall, answering the call for liberty, joined the Maryland militia.

Shortly after, Sarah took flight. But this time she headed north, not south.

Sarah had little sympathy for the colonists' cause. In her heart, she was still a royal princess. To support the rebels would directly conflict with that role.

Sarah met and married a young British lieutenant named William Stirling who served in the army of General William Howe. She followed Stirling in the Howe campaigns in New York and New Jersey. When Howe's forces entered Philadelphia late in September, 1777, Sarah was only a step behind her husband. The couple remained in Philadelphia until mid-1778.

After the surrender of the British in 1781, Sarah and her husband decided to remain in the United States. Were Sarah to have returned to England, she would have risked arrest and imprisonment.

The couple settled in New York City. Sarah still had a handsome sum of money that she had accumulated during her career as a princess, and she contributed what she had saved toward starting her husband in business as a ship's chandler, furnishing the equipment and supplies required by the many sailing vessels that entered the port of New York.

In the late 1700s and early 1800s, New York experienced amazing growth, gaining rank as the new nation's largest seaport. As the city grew, the Stirlings prospered, becoming one of New York's wealthiest families. They owned a large house in the most fashionable part of the city. Sarah had several servants at her beck and call. Thus, much of what Sarah had sought in her pose as a royal princess she eventually attained in her own right.

Chapter 4

Lord
Gordon-Gordon

In the decades following the Civil War, America resounded from one coast to the other with the construction of railroads. Thousands of miles of roadbed were laid down each year. By the beginning of the 1900s, the country was crisscrossed with steel rails. Even the smallest towns were linked into the huge network.

The period of greatest railroad construction was also a period of financial frenzy. Enormous sums of money had to be raised for the acquisition of land, laying of track, construction of bridges and stations, and the purchase of engines, cars, and the countless other pieces of required equipment.

It was the perfect setting for financial fraud and manipulation. Lord John Gordon-Gordon, who proclaimed himself to be a former member of the British Parliament and a trusted friend of the Queen's, surely realized this when he arrived in Minneapolis, Minnesota, in the spring of 1863. After registering at the city's finest hotel and depositing fifty thousand dollars in a local bank, Lord Gordon-Gordon began introducing himself to leading citizens of the area, announcing to one and all that he had come to Minneapolis to invest in new railroads.

To say that Lord Gordon-Gordon was welcomed is to be guilty of an understatement. He was given an enthusiastic reception. It is not difficult to understand why. Lord Gordon-Gordon was a tall, lean gentleman with a ready smile and meticulous manners. His mode of dress always included gray suede gloves, patent leather boots, and a tall silk hat. He presented letters of introduction from some of England's most noted statesmen to the bankers and brokers of Minneapolis. It was assumed by everyone that he was a socially prominent figure and extremely wealthy.

In reality, Lord Gordon-Gordon had no social standing whatsoever. What money he had was stolen. Lord Gordon-Gordon was an impostor.

He had been born Phillip Guy, the son of a merchant seaman and a London barmaid. As a boy, he obtained his pocket money by stealing dockside goods from ships that were being loaded or unloaded, and selling the merchandise to crooked pawnbrokers.

As Philip grew older, his thefts got bigger. One day he stole a trunk that was resting on a pier near a docked passenger ship. When he took the trunk home, broke open the lock, and peered inside, a frown crossed his face. The trunk contained a gentleman's wardrobe. It would not bring very much money at the pawnshop, Philip thought.

He removed a black satin coat from the trunk and tried it on. It fit perfectly. More for his amusement than anything else, he decked himself out in the gentleman's outfit. When he looked at himself in the mirror, he felt transformed. He did not merely look like a gentleman, he *was* a gentleman.

The masquerade was even more exhilarating when he walked the streets of London. People gave him the right of way and held doors for him when he entered buildings. Everywhere he went he was treated as a person of worth and excellence. He knew he could never go back to being Philip Guy again.

He began calling himself Lord Glencairn. He had calling cards and stationery printed bearing his name. He visited the clubs and coffee houses where gentlemen of the day gathered, and he studied them carefully, imitating their ways. He took to wearing thick sideburns in the fashion of the day and carrying a walking stick.

Philip soon hit upon a method of making his masquerade pay rich dividends. He entered the store of one of London's leading jewelers, presented his card, and asked to be shown various items. He selected one of the more expensive pieces and paid for it by check. The check was good, backed by money that he had accumulated during his career as a dock thief.

Lord Glencairn made purchases at other jewelry shops, paying by check. He made sure the checks were good. At the end of the week, Lord Glencairn took his purchases to Edinburgh in Scotland and pawned them. He was in London the next Monday, using the money from the pawned jewels to make more purchases.

The jewelry dealers of London looked upon Lord Glencairn as a godsend. They would rush to meet him as he entered their shops. They laid out their finest merchandise for his examination. When he began to receive this kind of treatment, Lord Glencairn knew it was time to strike.

In one frantic day, Lord Glencairn made sizable purchases in ten different London jewelry shops. He paid for the jewels by check. These checks were *not* good. Then Lord Glencairn vanished — and so did more than a million dollars in gems.

That night Philip tossed Lord Glencairn's wardrobe into the Thames River. The next day, he booked passage on a ship bound for America. When he arrived in New York, his first stop was a pawnship where he converted some of the stolen jewelry into cash. His next stop was a clothing store. There he purchased men's finery that would enable him to play the role of Lord John Gordon-Gordon.

At the time Lord Gordon-Gordon arrived in Minneapolis, the Northern Pacific Railroad was seeking to establish itself as a transcontinental line, linking the Great Lakes region with Portland, Oregon and Seattle, Washington. Enormous sums of money were required to do this.

Officials of the Northern Pacific Railroad approached Lord Gordon-Gordon. Would he be interested in investing in the railroad, they wanted to know, providing the funds that could be used for the purchase of land?

The officials arranged for Lord Gordon-Gordon to view the territory they wanted him to buy. They provided him with several expensive wagons for the tour, each fitted out and staffed with servants so as to provide him the utmost in personal comfort. Festive meals of the finest foods were served. In each of the cities and towns he called upon, Lord Gordon-Gordon was treated as a royal visitor.

The tour lasted three months. Then Lord Gordon-Gordon signed the papers that enabled him to purchase almost one million acres of land at a price that was somewhat less than a dollar an acre.

Lord Gordon-Gordon did not hold on to his land for very long. He traded his ownership rights for one million shares of stock in the Erie Railroad.

Some of the executives of the Erie were attempting to divert company funds into their own pockets by legal trickery. When he returned to New York, where headquarters for the Erie were located, Lord Gordon-Gordon managed to thwart the scheme. He became a hero in the eyes of leading Wall Street investors of the day.

One of these was millionaire Jay Gould, a member of the board of directors of several leading corporations and banks. Lord Gordon-Gordon went to Jay Gould and asked him to put money into the Erie corporation. He told him that if Gould were to make a substantial investment in the Erie, he would see to it that he became president of the company. Together he and Gould could continue the westward expansion of the Erie to the Pacific coast.

Gould agreed to invest several million dollars in the Erie, although he realized that the success of the venture depended largely on the cooperation and good faith of Lord Gordon-Gordon. When the financial world learned that Jay Gould was investing in the Erie Railroad, the company's stock shot up in value. That was exactly what Lord Gordon-Gordon had been waiting for. He began selling the shares he owned, reaping enormous profits. This caused a drop in prices.

Jay Gould became suspicious. At first, he could not prove it was Lord Gordon-Gordon who was dumping his stock. Then he realized that no one else owned so many shares. It *had* to be Lord Gordon-Gordon.

It was then that Gould fully realized that Lord Gordon-Gordon had tricked him. The two men eventually ended up in court, with Jay Gould claiming that Lord Gordon-Gordon had misrepresented himself and encouraged him to invest his money under false pretenses.

During the trial, Lord Gordon-Gordon's background came under scrutiny. He tried to turn aside all direct questions, saying only that he was a gentleman of breeding, highly regarded in the social and financial circles of London.

Jay Gould compiled a list of the individuals that Lord Gordon-Gordon claimed to know. He sent cablegrams to them all, asking them to attest to their friendship with Lord Gordon-Gordon. The replies were all the same. Nobody ever heard of him.

Lord Gordon-Gordon had learned what Jay Gould had done. On the day that he was to be revealed as an impostor, he did not appear in court. During the night, he had fled across the border into Canada. He took more than half a million dollars in cash and securities with him.

In Canada, Lord Gordon-Gordon sought to execute the same type of hoax he had performed in the United States. He traveled the country from east to west and back, saying that he was an investor looking for railroad properties to purchase.

American authorities had notified Canadian police to be on the lookout for Lord Gordon-Gordon. He was arrested before he had a chance to dupe anyone.

While Canadian and American law enforcement officials were confident they had an impostor in custody, it was widely held by the general public that Lord Gordon-Gordon was a British financier and man of social position. The police were unsure about what to do. Should Lord Gordon-Gordon be released or brought to trial?

While the debate was going on, Lord Gordon-Gordon's story and picture appeared in the London newspapers. The ten jewelers who had been flimflammed out of a million dollars in gems read the story and went to the police. Many of them produced the worthless checks they had been given by Lord Glencairn many years before. London police called their counterparts in the United States.

Lord Gordon-Gordon was brought before a judge. The charges against him involving fraudulent stock manipulation were read. Bail was set at one hundred thousand dollars. His lawyer produced the bail money and Lord Gordon-Gordon was free to go home.

That night Lord Gordon-Gordon skipped, never to be heard of again. Undoubtedly he assumed a new identity in another country, and spent his final days living by his cleverness and guile, always dressing in the height of fashion.

Chapter 5

The
Counterfeit Count

Victor Lustig was one of the most brilliant swindlers of all time. Throughout his life, he masqueraded as a count. He played the role to the hilt, always dressing stylishly and displaying perfect manners. "Confidence" and "charm" were two words always used in describing him.

Only once in his long career of crime did Lustig step out of character, taking part in a scheme that was more suited for a petty criminal. It was a blunder that cost him heavily. His one mistake balanced the scales of justice for all time.

Victor Lustig was born in 1890 in the small town of Hostinne in what is now Czechoslovakia. As a child growing up, he learned to speak both Czech and German. At boarding school in Germany, where he was sent when he reached high-school age, he was taught English, French, and Italian.

He liked languages. They were his favorite subject, in fact, and he got high marks in them.

Otherwise, school didn't interest Victor. He was a lazy pupil.

After his final year of boarding school, Victor was sent to Paris. His father believed that Victor was attending the University of Paris and sent him a monthly allowance.

But what Victor was really studying was gambling, and he was making plans to become a professional gambler. Bridge and poker were his favorite card games. He also enjoyed billiards and was highly skilled at it.

In time, Victor got so he could make a deck of cards do about anything but talk. He started "working the liners," sailing the great transatlantic ships of the time, playing cards or other gambling games with the passengers, some of whom were among the wealthiest people of the day. At the end of every Atlantic crossing, Victor would have a big bankroll.

It was during this period that Victor started calling himself a count. It was a perfect cover. Few people would ever suspect a member of the nobility of being a card shark.

World War I put an end to transatlantic travel by passenger ships. Lustig settled down in Paris to sit out the war. When peace came, he took up residence in the United States.

During his first winter in America, Lustig shuttled between Miami and the plush gambling casinos of Havana, representing himself as a producer of Broadway shows. He let it be known that he sometimes accepted money for investment in his productions.

Several people approached him and offered to participate in his ventures, but the sums they mentioned were too small for Lustig to bother about. He brushed them aside, waiting for a bigger fish to come along.

The fish took the form of a well-to-do, middle-aged shoe manufacturer from New Haven, Connecticut. He had always been interested in the stage, he told Lustig, and had once thought he could have been successful as an actor. Would Lustig accept some money from him for one of his productions?

Lustig explained that he was currently preparing a musical for Broadway and that musicals were expensive. This one was going to cost one hundred thousand dollars. Lustig said that he was putting up one-third of that amount himself, and he was looking for two other investors who would pledge similar sums.

"I'll put up a third," said the shoe manufacturer. "I'd love to be involved in a Broadway musical."

"But I don't like to accept money from friends," said Lustig. "What if the show flops? Not only does one lose money, but one can jeopardize a friendship as well."

The man insisted. Lustig shrugged. "If that's what you really want," he said. They agreed to meet at Lustig's hotel in New York the following week, at which time the man would deliver the money.

The man appeared at the appointed time. "This is the way we do it in show business," said Lustig, and he opened his suitcase and took out thirty-three thousand-dollar bills (which were counterfeit). "This is my share of the investment," he said.

Then the man took an envelope from his pocket and handed it to Lustig, who counted out the money it contained. "Thirty-three thousand dollars — fine!" Lustig said. Then he put each pile of money in an envelope, marked them, put the envelopes in his suitcase, and placed the suitcase on a shelf in his closet.

"Now for some dinner," said Lustig. The two men went to the hotel dining room.

They had just ordered when a bellman from the hotel appeared to tell the count he had a telephone call. "That must be my casting director," he said, excusing himself. "I'll be back in one minute."

But Lustig did not come back. After about a half hour, the shoe manufacturer called the count's room. There was no answer. Then he learned that Lustig had checked out. Of course, he had taken his suitcase with him.

The cheated man called the police. When they could not find Lustig, he hired private detectives to try and track him down. All of this made life a bit uncomfortable for Lustig, so he returned to Europe for several months.

Lustig was not always as successful as he had been with the shoe manufacturer. But when he did make a mistake, he never failed to learn from it. Over the years, he compiled a list of eight rules that he followed in his dealings with those individuals that he intended to victimize. They were as follows:

- Be a patient listener.
- Wait for the other man to reveal his political opinions, then agree with him.

- Wait for the other man to reveal his religious beliefs, then express similar ones.
- Never discuss ailments unless the other man is especially interested.
- Never pry into personal matters.
- Never brag.
- Never be untidy.
- Never get drunk.

During the winter of 1923, the count took up residence in Palm Beach, Florida, a city populated by countless millionaires. He acquired a Rolls Royce and employed a uniformed chauffeur to drive it.

With his charming accent and quaint, old-world manners, the count made friends quickly. He appraised each of his new acquaintances carefully, looking for a victim, a "mark."

Eventually he turned one up in the person of George Loller, a former mechanic who had become wealthy during World War I as a manufacturer of automobile and truck parts. Since arriving in Palm Springs aboard his huge yacht, he had been spending money in great amounts. But the count had learned that Loller's company had fallen on hard times, and he was being pressed for money from many directions. To the count, George Loller seemed the perfect person for the Romanian Box trick.

The count never failed to carry a Romanian Box with him. It was a moneymaker in every sense of the word.

Over the next week, the count did everything he could to become friendlier with Loller. One day he revealed to him that his family had lost its wealth as a result of World War I, a tale that never failed to get a sympathetic hearing. But, the count explained, he had hit upon a foolproof way of making a good living.

Loller's ears picked up when he heard that. "What is it?" he wanted to know. The count refused to say.

For several days, the count turned aside Loller's efforts to question him. Then, at what he felt was the appropriate moment, he told Loller that he had a machine that produced paper money.

From Loller's openmouthed reaction, the count knew that he had taken the hook. Now all he had to do was reel him in.

"Come to my hotel room," the count said. "I'll show you how it's done."

Once inside the room, the count locked the door and drew the blinds. Then he took from his suitcase a small, beautifully lacquered box, about the size of a shoebox. It was fitted with shiny brass knobs, glass-faced dials, and had slots on two sides, each slightly larger in width than a piece of paper money. As Loller stared at the box, the count reeled off an elaborate tale about its inventor and how the box had come into his possession.

Then the count proceeded to show Loller how the box worked. He took from his billfold a thousand-dollar bill. He handed it to Loller and asked him to examine it carefully, as well as a piece of blank paper the same size as the bill.

After adjusting the knobs and setting the dials, the count inserted the bill in one side of the box, and the blank piece of paper in the other. A complex chemical process was going to take place inside the box, the count explained, and the image on the bill would be transferred to the blank paper, but the original bill would not be changed in appearance.

The process would take four hours, said the count. The two spent the time aboard Loller's yacht, drinking and dining.

When they returned to the hotel room, the count fiddled with the knobs and dials again. Then he pulled a small lever, and out of the slots came two thousand-dollar bills.

Loller gasped in amazement. When he examined them, he saw that each of the bills had the same serial number — 24005688. What Loller didn't know was that the count, employing a master forger, had turned the threes on one of the bills into eights.

Loller begged the count to sell him the magical box, which would solve his financial problems for all time. The count, with seeming reluctance, agreed to take twenty-five thousand dollars for it.

When the box was his, Loller rushed to his yacht to try it out. It didn't work the first time, spewing out only the bill he had inserted. He tried it again with similar results. After a third unsuccessful try, Loller broke open the box to find it contained only a pair of rubber rollers and pieces of blank, bill-sized paper.

Loller sped to the count's hotel. The count had disappeared, of course. And, as far as Loller was concerned, the twenty-five thousand dollars had disappeared, too.

In the spring of 1925, Lustig returned to Paris, staying at the Crillon, one of the city's finest hotels. He now had an associate, a con man named

"Dapper Dan" Collins. The count never failed to introduce Dapper Dan as his private secretary.

One day the count came upon a story in his morning newspaper that sparked his interest. It said that the Eiffel Tower was in desperate need of repairs. The cost of the work would be several hundred thousand francs. Some government officials, feeling the expenditures were not worthwhile, stated it would be better to tear the tower down.

A smile crossed the count's face as he read the story. "We're going into the scrap iron business," he said to Dapper Dan. "Read this! All we need are a few letterheads and the right credentials."

A few weeks later, several scrap iron dealers assembled in a conference room at the Hotel Crillon. Each had been invited to the meeting by a letter from the Minister of Buildings and Monuments of the City of Paris for the purpose of discussing a contract.

Lustig, abandoning his identity as a count, introduced himself as a government official. He explained to the businessmen that the government was planning to take down the Eiffel Tower and sell its seven thousand tons of iron as scrap.

The men were shocked into silence by the news. "I'm telling you this in the strictest confidence," Lustig said. Then he went on to describe the famous tower in glowing detail, proclaiming its iron to be of the finest quality. "The highest bidder," Lustig continued, "will be favored with the contract."

The next morning, as Lustig had requested, the bids were delivered to his hotel in sealed envelopes. The envelope from Monsieur Jacques

Burlot was the only one that interested Lustig. He had already selected Burlot as his mark.

He instructed Dapper Dan to visit Burlot and inform him that his bid had been accepted. When Dan returned, he reported that Burlot seemed pleased with the news, but that he seemed somehow uneasy about the deal.

"Perhaps he does not believe we are government officials," Lustig said. "We'll have to prove that we are."

He told Dapper Dan to invite Burlot to a private meeting at the hotel. "Tell him," said Lustig, "the matter to be discussed is so private that I could not see him at my office."

Monsieur Burlot knew the reason for the meeting. It was no surprise to him when Lustig spent most of the evening complaining about the insecurity of his job, how it was put in jeopardy with every change of administration. He grumbled about his small salary and how much it cost him to dress well and do the entertaining that was expected of him.

Monsieur Burlot nodded in agreement. "I understand. I understand," he said. "I've dealt with civil servants before." He reached into his pocket, took out a roll of bills, and slipped it to Lustig.

When Burlot left that evening, Lustig knew that he had erased any doubts that he might have had. And, just as Lustig expected, a check from Burlot in payment for the Eiffel Tower scrap iron arrived within a few days. In return, Burlot received an official-looking document on government stationery, attesting to the fact that the iron contained in the Eiffel Tower was his.

Even before Burlot received his handsome document, Lustig and Dapper Dan, having cashed Burlot's check, were making their getaway. With Dapper Dan at the wheel of Lustig's car, they crossed into Germany and kept going until they reached Austria. They took up residence at one of Vienna's better hotels, spending a month there.

Every day Lustig would scan the Paris newspapers to see whether Burlot had gone to the police to report that he had been victimized. But he never did.

Two years later, Lustig was back in Paris, and he repeated the scheme. This time, however, the victim raced to the police when he realized that the "government official" had skipped with the money.

Lustig was in a faraway city when he read that the victim had gone to the police. The news saddened him. He knew it would be very difficult to sell the Eiffel Tower again.

When Lustig went back to the United States, the newspapers were filled with stories about Al Capone, the gang leader and racketeer whose syndicate terrorized Chicago and much of the Midwest. The stories never failed to appeal to Lustig. It would be interesting to meet Capone, he thought. Then it occurred to him it would be even more fascinating to try to con the mob leader. It would be the challenge of challenges. If he succeeded, Lustig knew it would give him enormous satisfaction. The thought of failing never crossed his mind.

The count had a simple method of getting to meet Capone. One summer afternoon, he planted himself outside the Hawthorne Inn in Chicago, headquarters for Capone and his gangland colleagues. He had spent only about five minutes staring up at the Inn's steel-barred windows when the front door opened and out came one of Capone's bodyguards.

"Don't hang around here," the man said.

"I am Count Victor Lustig. I want to see Al Capone."

"What about?"

"It is a private matter."

The guard went back inside, leaving Lustig on the sidewalk. A few minutes later, he returned, asked to see some identification. After he had searched Lustig for a weapon, he led him inside.

Lustig was brought to Capone's office and motioned to take a seat before the mob leader's desk. Capone studied Lustig, not saying a word.

The count didn't wait for an invitation to begin, but launched into an explanation of what he described as a "very unusual investment opportunity." With the help of some Wall Street friends, he said, it was possible for him to double any amount of money entrusted to him, and do it within sixty days.

The count could sense that he was making a favorable impression upon Capone with his cultured speech, fine clothes, and confident manner. He became even more glib and assured.

When the count paused to get a reaction to what he had been saying, Capone asked, "What's the minimum?"

"Fifty thousand dollars," said the count.

Capone opened a drawer in his desk, took out a bundle of thousand-dollar bills, counted out fifty of them, and pushed them across the desk to the count. "I don't throw money out the window," Capone said. "When I go into business, I don't fool around. Watch this." Capone pressed a button and a panel in the wall on one side of the room slid open, and there stood a man, pistol in hand, his finger on the trigger.

"Understand?" said Capone.

"Yes," said Lustig with a smile, "I understand."

Getting the fifty thousand dollars from Capone had not been hard. Keeping it was going to be the difficult part. Lustig had no double-your-money scheme. It was something he had made up on the spur of the moment.

One thing he knew for sure: he was not going to spend any of Capone's money. He deposited it in a bank.

When the sixty days were up, Lustig did nothing. He did not try to hide; in fact, he did the opposite, showing himself frequently in bars and restaurants where he knew Capone's men would be.

About a month after the deadline had passed, a bartender told Lustig that Capone was looking for him. The next day the count drove out to the Hawthorne Inn and asked to see Capone. He was searched and brought inside.

There was no exchange of greetings. "You're weeks late," Capone snapped. "What's going on?"

Lustig put on a mournful face. "I'm terribly sorry," he said. "I had some trouble. Nothing worked out the way I wanted it to."

Capone leaned back in his chair and fixed Lustig in a chilly stare. As Lustig started to unfold his long tale of grief, he could see Capone's face getting redder and redder. Suddenly Capone leaped to his feet, slammed a fist on the desk, and shouted out, "What about the money? Have you got my money?"

"Oh, yes, sir," said Lustig. He took an envelope from his pocket, opened it, and counted out fifty thousand dollars.

Nothing could have jolted Capone more. He had felt certain that Lustig had either lost or spent the money, and he had been expecting to hear a sorrowful apology and plea for time in which to pay the money back.

"This is most embarrassing for me, Mr. Capone," said Lustig. "I would like to have earned a profit for you — and for myself as well. I need it, you know."

As Lustig got up as if to leave, Capone said, "Wait a minute. Are you in some kind of a jam?"

Lustig nodded. "Well, in fact, yes, I am."

Capone reached toward the stack of bills and picked five from the top of the pile. "Will this help?" he said.

"It certainly will," said the Count. "I'm most grateful, sir. Thank you very much."

As he was leaving, the count had to fight back a self-satisfied grin. He had challenged the gangster king — and won.

By the early 1930s, the count had rolled up some impressive statistics. He had played twenty-three different roles in fleecing people and had been arrested forty-seven times. But because his victims seldom came forward to testify against him, the Count had never been convicted or jailed for any extended time.

The count's good fortune changed in 1934. A

master forger named William Watts employed the count to distribute counterfeit money. The count was highly skilled at it. Treasury agents estimated that one hundred thousand dollars a month in phony money was being put into circulation in the Northeast. A special squad of Secret Service agents was organized to find the counterfeiters.

The trail led to an apartment house in Union City, New Jersey, where Watts was found at work with his engraving tools. Police found many thousands of dollars in forged money in the apartment.

Watts told the truth about the operation and how Lustig had helped him. In December, 1935, the two men were placed on trial in New York. Watts was sentenced to fifteen years. The count's sentence was twenty years.

The count spent the last years of his life in Alcatraz. No longer did he display confidence and charm. He became quiet and melancholy, and often spent hours sitting on his bunk staring at the floor.

He saw only one friend from the prosperous days of the past. He worked in the laundry. His name was Al Capone.

Chapter 6

The Claimant

Some impostors assume a good number of names and identities throughout their lives. Fred Demara is the prime example. But there are others who play only one role through their entire lifetime. This chapter concerns an impostor of that type.

His name was Arthur Orton. He engaged in a lifelong struggle to prove that he was Sir Roger Tichborne, heir to an enormous fortune. He not only succeeded in getting millions of people to believe him, but he cost one of England's richest and most renowned families a fortune to defend what was rightly theirs. And he cost the British government huge sums in their efforts to convict him. The case has been called "the most extraordinary imposture in the history of mankind."

Sir Charles Doughty Tichborne, a wealthy English baron, and the head of a family that owned huge tracts of land in England for many years, died unexpectedly, leaving no children. The baron's sixteen-year-old nephew, Roger Tichborne, was named heir to his uncle's title and great wealth.

Roger had been born and raised in France. After his uncle's death, he and his parents moved to England. Roger became a student at Stonyhurst, a well-known boarding school of the day. When he turned twenty, Roger entered the military service, obtaining a commission in the Sixth Dragoon Guards.

Not long after, Roger fell deeply in love with Katherine Doughty, a girl of eighteen, and his first cousin. They made plans to marry.

But Roger's mother and father, and Katherine's parents, too, opposed the marriage. The families were Catholic, and the Catholic Church forbids marriages between first cousins.

"Wait three years," Roger's father told him. "If you and Katherine still want to marry, I will give my blessing."

It was a difficult decision for Roger, but he agreed to wait the three-year period. Katherine, seeing that there was no other solution, agreed to wait, too.

To help make the time pass quickly, Roger decided he would travel the world. On the last day that he and Katherine were together, Roger produced a letter that he had written to her. He asked her to read it and make a copy of it in her own hand. Then he gave the letter to a friend to keep.

The letter was to play an important part in the events that were to come. It read: "I make on this day a promise that if I marry my cousin, Katherine Doughty, before three years are over, I will build a church or chapel at Tichborne to the Holy Virgin in thanksgiving for the protection which

55

she has thrown over us, and in praying God that our wishes may be fullfilled."

Roger's adventuring first took him to South America. After spending several months there, he sailed from Rio de Janeiro for Australia aboard a small British ship, the *Bella*.

The *Bella* disappeared in a storm. Except for a logbook found floating some 400 miles from land, no trace of the vessel was ever seen again.

Three years later, a court of law in England pronounced Roger officially dead. His younger brother, Alfred, inherited the family wealth that would have gone to him. When Alfred died at the age of twenty-seven, his infant son fell heir to the fortune.

These events turned Roger's mother, Lady Tichborne, into a tragic figure. A highly emotional and strong-willed woman, she had always had her way with her husband, with Roger, and with virtually everyone else. She could not accept the fact that Roger, the oldest and most beloved of her children, was really dead.

Some years after the disappearance of the *Bella*, Lady Tichborne began advertising in newspapers in distant countries for news of her son. Papers in Australia were among those that carried the advertisement.

In the small Australian town of Wagga Wagga, a butcher named Arthur Orton saw the advertisement. Early in 1866, Orton wrote to Lady Tichborne, addressing her as "My dear Mother," and explaining that he was her lost son.

When Lady Tichborne received the letter, it was as if all her prayers had been answered. "My dearest and beloved Roger," she said in her reply,

"I have never lost hope of seeing you again in this world." The letter went on to rejoice at Roger's well-being.

Lady Tichborne's enthusiastic response was more than Orton had hoped for. When he had written to her, he did so with the motive of getting some small sum of money from her. But now he realized that a bigger opportunity was at hand. He decided to press his claim as far as he possibly could.

Orton was not a well-educated man. His wife, an Australian servant girl, could neither read nor write. But Orton was clever and quick-witted, and developed the knack of feeding back information to Lady Tichborne that had originally been provided by her, and doing it in such a way that she believed *he* was the source.

When Lady Tichborne informed Orton that Alfred and his father had died, Orton's reply was filled with laments for "my poor father" and "my dear brother Alfred."

Then the letter continued, "I hardly know, my dear Mother, how you have borne the suspense of not knowing my fate for so long. You must not blame me, for I believe that fate had a great deal to do with it."

In her next letter, Lady Tichborne told Orton of a former servant of the family's that was now living in Sydney. The servant's name was Bogle. "He will know you, Roger," Lady Tichborne said.

This was first of countless challenges Orton was to face over the next few years, and he prepared for it carefully, memorizing all of the facts about the family that had been set down in Lady Tichborne's letters.

When he went to visit the elderly Bogle, he greeted him by name and embraced him warmly. Before Bogle could come to any understanding of the situation, Orton assailed him with information about the death of his "poor father and dear Alfred." By the time he left, Bogle was convinced that Orton was Roger Tichborne. He wrote to Lady Tichborne and told her how thrilled he had been to see Roger and talk to him.

Lady Tichborne needed no additional evidence. She sent Orton the money he needed for his passage to England. He brought his wife, two children, and Bogle with him.

When Roger Tichborne had left England a decade before, he was of smallish build and medium height, weighing 125 pounds. He had a long, thin face, sandy, straight hair, and a tattoo. Since he had lived in France until he was sixteen, and had gone to school there, he spoke French fluently.

Orton, by contrast, weighed 280 pounds, had a big, round face, and dark, wavy hair. He had no tattoo. He spoke only English.

But so deeply did Lady Tichborne want to believe that the Wagga Wagga butcher was her son, that she accepted him immediately. She also provided him and his family with a handsome living allowance.

Orton was thrilled by his quick success. Dreams of a life of ease began to dance in his head. But not for long. Lady Tichborne sent for a former teacher of Roger's, Henri Chatillon. When introduced to Orton, Chatillon spoke to him in French, the language they had always used together.

Orton's brow wrinkled. He had not the slightest idea what Chatillon was saying.

Chatillon then switched to English, but only to tell Orton that he did not believe that he was Roger Tichborne. It was Orton's first clue as to the struggle he was to face.

Orton read all he could about the Tichborne family, and memorized every fact he thought might ever be of the tiniest importance. He became friendly with Robert Hopkins, the family lawyer, and he scored a significant victory by convincing Hopkins that he was the rightful heir to the Tichborne fortune.

Orton and Hopkins discussed the Tichbornes' family affairs in the greatest detail. Using information that he had obtained from Hopkins, Orton called on several of the family's neighbors. He chatted with them about old friends and times past, and by so doing persuaded some of them that he was Roger.

Orton's next move was to befriend some of the old soldiers in the Sixth Dragoon Guards, the military regiment in which Roger had served. Two of them he invited to stay at his home. He spent long evenings talking with the soldiers, encouraging them to tell him all they knew of Roger's military career. Then he invited other soldiers to visit him, and followed the same procedure.

Once he felt sufficiently informed, Orton called upon some of Roger's fellow officers. Some of these soon believed that Orton was Roger Tichborne.

Now came a stern test for Orton. Roger's closest friend had been Vincent Gosport. Roger had given Vincent the letter he had shown to Katherine and which she had copied, the letter that had contained the promise that he would build a chapel if they were married.

Gosport was eager to see his old friend. When he met Orton and the two men chatted, Gosport was impressed with all he knew about the old days. He seemed almost ready to accept him.

But then Gosport asked him about the sealed letter Roger had given him before he left England. "What was in the letter?" Gosport asked.

The impostor thought for a moment. "I don't remember," he said.

To Gosport, this was an important test, and this man had failed it. Gosport was convinced the man was an impostor.

But Orton didn't care what Gosport thought. He was too deeply committed. There could be no turning back. Instead, he moved ahead boldly.

Orton swore out official papers at the Chancery Division of the court, where such matters as wills and estates are handled, claiming he was Sir Roger Tichborne. He requested the court to turn over to him the money and property that had been left to Henry Tichborne, the son of his dead brother Alfred.

In his statement, Orton provided a long account of rescue from the wreck of the *Bella*. Eight other seamen survived with him, Orton said. They were rescued by a passing ship, the *Osprey*, and taken to Melbourne.

When Orton was cross-examined, he badly damaged his cause, revealing great gaps of information. Yes, he admitted, he had spent his boyhood in France, but he spoke no French. He could not remember the names of any of his boyhood friends. When questioned about Stonyhurst, the school he had attended in England for two years, he could not recall the names of any of his teachers nor give the title of even one book he had read as a student.

Then it was Vincent Gosport's turn to take the stand. He told about the sealed envelope Roger had given him at the time of his departure. He did not reveal the contents of the letter, saying only that it concerned Katherine Doughty. Vincent stated that he had destroyed the letter after learning of Roger's death.

The lawyer for the Tichborne family recalled Orton to the stand to question him about the letter and its contents. Orton had no idea what the letter had said, so he had to invent something. The tale he spun was further evidence of his cleverness and callousness.

He had written the letter, Orton declared, after Katherine had told him that she was pregnant, and had begged him to marry her. He did not believe that she was pregnant, but was only claiming to be so she could get him to marry her. If, however, it turned out to be true, then Gosport was to arrange for Katherine to leave England, and the letter contained instructions he was to follow.

Gasps filled the courtroom. The judge's mouth hung open. In Victorian England, such matters were not the subject of public discussion.

By this time, much of England had been drawn into the case, with passions heated on both sides. Many people turned against Orton as a result of his statement that Katherine had been less than virtuous. One newspaper of the day declared, "A blacker lie was never committed to paper, and a more diabolical plot was never formed in the heart of man."

The hearing was adjourned to give both sides time to gather and assemble more evidence. During the period of adjournment, Lady Tichborne died, as did Robert Hopkins, the family lawyer who had befriended Orton. Their deaths deprived Orton of two of his best witnesses.

The court hearing resumed early in 1871. Orton was quick to demonstrate how thoroughly he had prepared for it. His lawyer called a long succession of witnesses who testified in his behalf. They included soldiers of the Sixth Dragoon Guards, their officers, and a governess who had been employed by the Tichborne family.

Not only did these witnesses swear that the claimant was really Roger Tichborne, but each offered a different reason for making the identification. One cited "a peculiar expression of the eyes"; another, "wrinkles on his brow"; and still another, "dimples in his hands." In all, ninety witnesses paraded to the stand on Orton's behalf.

Then the lawyer for the Tichborne family took over. He called Katherine Doughty, now Mrs. J. R. Radcliffe, to the stand, and questioned her about the letter in the sealed envelope. In a barely audible voice, Katherine explained the letter contained Roger's promise to build a chapel should they marry. The courtroom was deathly quiet as Katherine spoke and the jury seemed genuinely moved by her testimony.

Two aunts of Roger's swore the claimant could not possibly be their nephew. Several other witnesses wanted to know what had become of the initials "R.T." that had been tattooed on Roger's right forearm.

The Tichborne lawyers had sent investigators to Australia to learn more about the supposed Roger Tichborne. They found out that his real name was Arthur Orton and that he was wanted by the police in Australia for stealing a horse.

Orton was then recalled to the witness stand. Again he showed terrible ignorance about Roger Tichborne's boyhood in Paris and various subjects he had studied in school at Stonyhurst. Asked to describe the drill procedure used by the Sixth Dragoons, Orton was forced to state that he knew nothing of it.

The lawyer then asked him how it was that he had not written to his family once during the many years he had spent in Australia. He answered that he had been working hard and his neglect stemmed from "carelessness."

After one hundred and two days, the hearing ended and the case was given to the jury. Quickly the jury brought back its verdict. The claimant was not Sir Roger Tichborne, they decided. He was an impostor.

The Chief Justice ordered the police to arrest Orton. He was charged with perjury and an attempt to defraud. He was taken to Newgate Prison.

When Orton arrived at the prison in police custody, a huge crowd had assembled to greet him. He grinned and waved. The crowd cheered him loudly. While he had been unable to convince a judge and jury that his cause was just, he had won thousands of supporters throughout England.

Known simply as "The Claimant," Arthur Orton had become a popular cause.

A criminal trial was scheduled on the charges that had been brought against him. But because witnesses were to be brought to England from Australia, the trial was delayed for many months. Orton was released on bail that was posted by his friends.

During the months he was free, Orton's public support grew by leaps and bounds. Donations flooded in to pay for defense. He spoke at public meetings and music halls. Everywhere he went, Orton was hailed as a hero.

Almost a year went by, and then the trial began. Enormous crowds packed the courtroom daily. The trial was very much a replay of hearings that had gone before, but with two important differences. One was the introduction of a man who claimed to be a crew member of the *Bella* and claimed he was in the lifeboat with Roger Tichborne when the vessel sank. He confirmed the claimant's story that they were rescued by the *Osprey* and taken to Melbourne.

This loomed as telling evidence for the claimant, but the Tichborne lawyer produced documents showing that the sailor who testified was in prison at the time the *Bella* sank. Since it could only be concluded that Orton had arranged the testimony, his case was damaged by it.

Orton was also hurt by the introduction of a notebook that had been brought from Australia that contained entries in what was said to be the claimant's handwriting. Although clumsily worded, one entry proved extremely harmful to Orton. It read: "Some men has plenty money and no brains, and some men has plenty brains and no money. Surely men with plenty money and no brains were made for men with plenty brains and no money."

The claimant said the notebook was not his. "It's a forgery," he declared.

At the trial's end, Dr. Edward Kenealy, the claimant's lawyer, pleaded at length for his client. According to one source, his summing-up speech took twenty-three days to deliver. The trial itself lasted one hundred eighty-eight days and was the longest trial in British courtroom history up to that time.

No one was surprised when the claimant was found guilty. He was handed a fourteen-year jail sentence.

With Orton in prison, Dr. Kenealy continued to whip up support for his cause. He addressed almost any public meeting that would hear him and published a weekly newspaper, *The Englishman*, that protested the persecution and imprisonment of "Sir Roger Tichborne." A society formed to support the cause of the claimant held meetings that attracted thousands.

In 1875, Dr. Kenealy ran for a seat in Parliament and won. Once a member of the government, he requested the forming of a Royal Commission to inquire into Orton's trial, but the idea received no support.

In time, Orton's cause began to bore people. When Kenealy ran for reelection, he was defeated. He died soon afterward.

Meanwhile, Arthur Orton, a model prisoner, was serving out his time. He was released in 1884.

Orton found that few people remembered his cause, and those who did remember had little interest in it. Nevertheless, he continued to represent himself as the claimant to the Tichborne fortune.

He lived in a tiny room in a cheap boarding house and held a series of menial jobs. He died in 1898. On his coffin, someone inscribed the name "Sir Roger Tichborne."

Chapter 7

The
Baron of Arizona

On May 9, 1881, every homesteader, rancher, and property owner in and near the city of Phoenix in what was then the Arizona Territory heard news that sent them reeling. A tall, slim, distinguished-looking gentleman named James Addison Reavis had appeared upon the scene to announce that he owned every square inch of a sizable chunk of what is today Arizona's Maricopa County. The land included the entire city of Phoenix, the adjacent towns of Tempe, Glendale, and Paradise Valley, and several others. Reavis posted handbills throughout the area announcing that landowners must come forward and render him sufficient sums of money or risk losing their property through court action.

Reavis probably would have been taken off to the nearest insane asylum were it not for the fact that he offered official documentation for his bizarre claim. The property was all his, he said, under the terms of a deed he had purchased in which the land had been granted to one Miguel de Peralta by a Spanish king.

Throughout the decade that followed, armies of lawyers struggled to resolve the dispute between Reavis and the Arizona landowners. At first, Reavis's claim was accepted, and he began negotiating huge settlements. But, in time, it was established that the Reavis documents were clever forgeries and the families that Reavis had offered as the original property owners existed only in his very active imagination.

Reavis spent years in the creating of his scheme. It actually had its beginning during the Civil War. Reavis, a Confederate soldier, forged his captain's signature onto a pass that enabled him to leave his post for several days. The guard at the gate never questioned the signature for a moment. Reavis worked the ruse again and again during his army career, forging the names of several different officers.

Reavis realized he had a talent for forgery. Just as some people can play the piano by ear, recreating a melody after hearing it only once or twice, Reavis had the ability to duplicate a person's signature after having studied it for only a short period. He spent some part of every day in developing his skill.

Reavis forged the base commander's signature to receipts for supplies delivered to the post. He would then sell the supplies and pocket the money.

Toward the end of his career in the army, Reavis created payroll records for soldiers and officers who never existed. Then he would cash payroll checks that he had made out bearing the names of the phantom men.

After the Civil War ended, Reavis was discharged from the army. He journeyed to Santa Fe, New Mexico, where he got a job in the record room of a government bureau investigating Spanish land claims. It had been the custom of Spanish kings to reward their favorite subjects with gifts of vast tracts of land in the New World. According to the Treaty of Guadalupe Hidalgo, signed in 1848, which set the terms of peace at the close of the Mexican War, the United States agreed to recognize Spanish titles to all lands within the newly acquired territory. The Gadsden Purchase, negotiated with Mexico in 1853, affirmed this right. When Arizona became a federal territory in 1863 and the movement for statehood began, land ownership claims were brought into sharp focus.

Reavis was aware of all of this, of course, as he toiled away amidst tall stacks of ancient Spanish documents. His plan was to forge documents that would establish him as the holder of a Spanish land grant.

But before he could set his pen to paper, Reavis had to create a family upon which he could base his fraud. His inventive mind produced Miguel de Peralta, a distant relative of King Ferdinand of Spain and a Knight of the Military Order of Carlos III. Miguel's father, as created by Reavis, was José Gaston Gomez de Silva y Montux de Oca; his mother, Doña Francesca Ana Maria Garcia de la Cordoba.

Once he had created a family tree, Reavis began working day and night preparing the documents that would give substance to his claim. He began by mastering the Spanish language, not merely as it existed in his day, but as it was spoken and written almost two hundred years before. He also became skilled in the use of quills, that is, feathers formed into pens for writing. He practiced with quills for weeks at a time, copying the script from centuries-old documents.

When he felt ready to commit his forgery to paper, Reavis first had to remove the names of the real landowners from the documents he chose to work with. Special chemicals enabled him to do this. The names of Miguel de Peralta and his fictitious ancestors were then inserted in the appropriate places.

Reavis then had to establish a legal link between the Peralta family and himself. He had become acquainted with George Willing, a local vagrant who lived off handouts and had no known family. Reavis prepared documents declaring that Willing had purchased from Miguel de Peralta all of Peralta's land holdings for the sum of one thousand dollars. Willing had later sold the land to Reavis for thirty thousand dollars, or so a document Reavis prepared stated. So it was that Reavis now claimed to have legal title to the land in question.

Not long after Reavis had prepared his documentation and planted the deeds among the official records of the Territory of Arizona, George Willing died under mysterious circumstances in the town of Prescott, Arizona. One source said that he died of poison. Prescott was a boisterous, lawless town in those days, and no one bothered investigating Willing's death.

When all of his documentation was ready, and Willing in no position to dispute matters, Reavis released his bombshell. His bold claim sent lawyers scurrying to the land claims office. The evidence was all there. There could be no mistake about it. The lawyers advised their clients to settle with Reavis.

The money began pouring in. A mining company paid Reavis twenty-five thousand dollars. The Southern Pacific Railroad came forth with fifty thousand dollars. Ranchers, farmers, and homeowners also contributed, giving Reavis amounts ranging from fifty to five hundred dollars. In the first year that followed the filing of his claim, Reavis collected almost half a million dollars. Seldom had imposture paid so well.

But that might have been only the beginning. The federal government had once been the biggest landowner in the area covered by the Peralta grant. In the years since the area had become an official territory, the government had deeded much of the land to homesteaders. Reavis wanted twenty-five million dollars from the federal government to make valid all of the homesteaders' deeds, and the government seriously considered paying him that amount.

Reavis soon took on the character and personality of a royal person. He called himself Don James Addison de Peralta-Reavis, Baron of Arizona. He owned a mansion in St. Louis and another in Washington. He bought a palace in Mexico and named it his official residence. He married a young Mexican servant girl, then invented ancestors for her in an effort to establish that she was a person of noble Spanish birth. When twin boys were born to the couple, he dressed them in red velvet, as if they were Spanish princes. When the baron, as he took to calling himself, the baroness, and their two children drove through the streets of Phoenix in their handsome carriage behind six white horses, people lined the streets to gape.

Year followed year, and no one came forward to question Reavis's claim. Not until 1890, when Royal Johnson, the surveyor-general for the Territory, completed an investigation, was a voice raised in serious opposition to Reavis. Johnson's report on the matter stated Reavis's claim was not legitimate. It failed to conform to historical facts, said Johnson, and was in all likelihood based on forgery.

The case was eventually placed in the hands of the U.S. Court of Private Land Grant claims. Court officers sent investigators to California and Mexico to reexamine the documents upon which Reavis based his title. They used chemicals to analyze the inks with which the documents had been prepared. The investigators found that certain pages of certain documents were written in dogwood ink, the type of ink then in general use. Iron ink had been the kind of ink in use at the time the documents had originally been prepared.

The investigators used other chemicals to remove the dogwood ink and bring back what had been written in iron ink. In the document granting Miguel de Peralta title to his huge tract of land, quite another name was made to appear.

The documents that had been prepared to show that Reavis's wife was of noble birth were also proved to be fraudulent. Reavis did not know that the padres who had prepared the birth records for the period in question had maintained a careful index of all births in a separate register. While Reavis had inserted a birth record for his wife in the files, he had made no entry in the index. Further investigation showed the birth document to be a forgery.

Reavis spent every cent he had in defending himself. But the government's case against him was much too strong. He was convicted of fraud and sentenced to six years in the federal penitentiary in Santa Fe. His wife and children fled to Denver, then disappeared.

Reavis was released from prison in 1901. By that time he was an old man, bearded and bent. He spent the last years of his life in the Phoenix public library, reading newspaper accounts about himself and his days of wealth and glory.

Chapter 8

The Actress

Constance Cassandra Chadwick was one of the most successful female impostors of all time. Her masquerades enabled her to swindle some of the most noted banks and brokerage houses of her day out of millions of dollars. "Goldbrick Cassie," she was nicknamed.

Cassie Chadwick was born in Toronto, Canada, in 1845, the oldest child in a family of eight children—four boys and four girls. Her parents were poor, hardworking people. Cassie dropped out of school at an early age to help in raising the children.

As a teenager, Cassie dreamed of the day she would be able to escape from the role into which she had been thrust. Her first job was as a clerk in a Toronto department store. The city's wealthiest women shopped there. Cassie envied their elegant clothes and fine manners. She realized that if she were ever to become a "socially acceptable" person, she would have to adopt the character and personality traits these women displayed.

Cassie was in her early twenties when she left Toronto and took up residence in New York City. She embarked on her career as an impostor not long after her arrival, masquerading as a noted spiritualist of the day, a woman who proclaimed to her followers that she could see into the future.

In this role, Cassie would announce to a wealthy man or woman that he or she was about to be brutally murdered by thieves intent upon robbery. "Transfer your holdings to me," Cassie would advise her victims. "Then the thieves will have no reason to assault or rob you." It never seemed to occur to her victims that the thieves had no way of knowing that they had gotten rid of their holdings. As soon as the transfer was made, Cassie converted everything to cash and dropped out of sight.

Cassie's swindles managed to net her many thousands of dollars. But for Cassie, who dreamed much loftier dreams, this was only the beginning.

Cassie loved to read. Her tastes ranged far and wide. In one of her reading sessions, she learned that New York society revolved around steel baron Andrew Carnegie, one of the most noted industrialists of the day. She read how Carnegie, who had been born in Scotland, was raised in poverty. He had to stuff newspapers into his shoes in order to be able to walk the several miles to the grocery store where he worked. He was paid, not in money, but in food, usually a few loaves of bread and fruit and vegetables that were on the brink of spoilage.

In all that she read of Carnegie, one sentence stood out. It flashed on and off in her mind like a neon sign. It read: "Just the mention of Andrew

Carnegie's name is sufficient to prompt any banker in the world to open his vaults."

That was an overstatement, of course, the product of some newspaperman's enthusiasm. But there was more than a grain of truth to it. In the financial world, no name was more exalted than that of Andrew Carnegie's. Overstatement or not, the line triggered an ingenious plan in Cassie's mind that could, in fact, prompt bankers to open their vaults, and perhaps even open them for her.

Over the next several months, Cassie read every word she could about Carnegie. Not only did she learn how he had gone about putting together his financial empire, which centered around steel production, and about his charitable zeal (he established more than 2,800 libraries in the United States), but she learned all she could about him personally — the type of clothes he wore, his preferences in food, and his favorite colors. She came to know all of his likes and dislikes, his mannerisms, and even the quirks of personality he had. For example, Carnegie had the doorways in his huge mansion on Fifth Avenue in New York constructed to accommodate only individuals of smallish size; Carnegie himself was a mere five feet six inches. Anyone taller had to stoop over to get through a Carnegie doorway. Cassie got to know all she could about that mansion, including the layout of each floor, where the various rooms were located, and who occupied which bedrooms. She came to know the names and a bit of background information concerning each of the servants that staffed the mansion.

"I put my real identity out of my mind," Cassie was to write in later years. "I wanted to forget my poor Toronto family, my very poor upbringing. All I wanted to know was that I was a favorite of Andrew Carnegie's, traveled with him, lived with him in his Fifth Avenue mansion in New York, and, in fact, performed all the duties of a very familiar friend."

Cassie was a striking figure now, perhaps at the very height of her beauty. She wore her red hair in a stylish upsweep, topped with beguiling ringlets. Her skin was smooth, white, flawless. The green earrings and necklace she frequently wore seemed to heighten the sparkle of her brilliant green eyes.

One afternoon after she had gotten settled in her hotel, she went to Delmonico's restaurant in New York for a light lunch. Located on the southern edge of Hanover Square in New York's financial district, and housed in a handsome brownstone building, Delmonico's was hemmed in on all sides by brokerage companies, bond houses, and investment firms. The New York Stock Exchange was also close by.

On entering the restaurant, Cassie was led to a table in the main-floor dining room. Out of the corner of her eye she noted that the men who were standing or seated at the long oak bar turned almost in unison to watch her. Cassie's intention in visiting Delmonico's was to meet a broker or investment banker who handled big stock and bond purchases.

When she was seated, she glanced about the room until her eyes rested upon a ticker, a glass-domed telegraphic receiving device that automatically printed stock prices on a paper tape. The ticker could be part of her plan, Cassie thought. It was not far from her table.

As Cassie sipped her tea and nibbled on a honey muffin, she noted that she had caught the attention of a distinguished-looking gentleman who kept glancing in her direction. He wore a dark cutaway coat over his white starched shirt with its high collar. His hair was neatly groomed and his side whiskers were carefully trimmed. If he was not a man of wealth, he was surely on his way to reaching that status.

It was time for Cassie to make her first move. Gathering up her skirts, she walked over to the ticker. She let the tape sift through her fingers as it spewed from the machine. She stared intently at the symbols and numbers. Suddenly she smiled broadly. In a voice that was loud enough for those nearby to hear, she said, "Mr. Carnegie is going to be very pleased."

As she turned to go back to her table, she saw she had been overheard by her prospective victim. "Oh, I'm sorry, sir," Cassie said. "I didn't mean to disturb you. It's just that I'm so excited. Mr. Carnegie took my advice, bought a stock at my suggestion, and it has gone up quite nicely. He is sure to be grateful."

The man rose politely. "I congratulate you on your good fortune," he said. "You are talking about *the* Mr. Carnegie, I assume."

Cassie nodded, then started to move back to her table. "Permit me to introduce myself," the man continued, offering her his business card. "I am Casper W. Swanberg, an investment banker."

Cassie gave her name in a soft voice. "Perhaps you will give me the pleasure of joining me for a bit of tea," Mr. Swanberg said.

A waiter dashed forward to pull out a chair at

Mr. Swanberg's table. "I don't have long," Cassie said as she seated herself. "I have an appointment I must go to."

They talked about business conditions and stock market process. Cassie injected Mr. Carnegie's name into the conversation at every opportunity.

"I must be leaving," she said at length, glancing at her watch. "It is Mr. Carnegie with whom I am meeting. We are having tea together. As you probably know, he does not like to be kept waiting."

"Perhaps you'd allow me to drop you there," Swanberg said.

Cassie readily agreed. Outside, Swanberg hailed a carriage, and instructed the driver to take them to Carnegie's home. As the carriage made its way up Broadway to Fifth Avenue, Cassie began spinning her web, explaining that she was a "very close friend" of Mr. Carnegie's and that he shared his investment plans with her. Swanberg could hardly suppress his excitement. It would be wonderful, he thought, if he could entice Cassie to reveal what stock purchases Mr. Carnegie planned. It was seldom that Mr. Carnegie made a poor investment. Knowing in advance what the industrialist planned to do could be of enormous advantage to Swanberg and the clients he represented.

When the carriage was within a few blocks of the mansion, Cassie asked, "Would you care to meet Mr. Carnegie? Perhaps I could arrange for you to join the two of us for tea."

Swanberg struggled to contain his delight. "That would be very kind of you, indeed, Miss Chadwick," he replied, allowing himself a smile.

As the carriage wheeled into the driveway in front of the Carnegie mansion and came to a stop, Swanberg was about to step down when Cassie placed her hand on his arm. "I think it would be wiser if I spoke to Mr. Carnegie first," she said, "and told him that a luncheon acquaintance of mine was eager to meet him. That would seem the proper thing to do. Would you mind remaining here? It will take only a few moments."

Swanberg had no choice. "I shall be happy to wait," he said.

Cassie smiled and left the carriage. It was only a few steps to the door. As she rang the bell, she could feel her heart pounding. Her role as an impostor was developing at a rapid clip. But Cassie was the picture of poise and confidence, knowing that she had prepared herself thoroughly for the events that were about to unfold.

A maid answered the door. "I telephoned to speak to the housekeeper," Cassie said. "May I see her, please?"

"Please follow me, ma'am," said the maid, and she led Cassie to the servants' parlor. When the housekeeper arrived, Cassie came right to the point.

"I'm about to hire a maid. Her name is René LeFlore. When I asked her for references, she told me she had once worked for Mr. Carnegie. Would you be good enough to advise me of her capabilities?"

The housekeeper's brow wrinkled. "I'm very sorry," she said. "I know of no René LeFlore. I don't recall anyone by that name ever working here."

Cassie feigned surprise. "Why, she even gave

me a letter of recommendation from Mr. Carnegie."

"May I see the letter?" said the housekeeper.

Cassie had no letter, of course. Saying that she did was part of her scheme to gain time. She started rummaging through her handbag, examining various letters and papers. The housekeeper looked on sympathetically. Finally, Cassie sighed in frustration. "How stupid!" she said. "I must have left the letter in another bag. But it really doesn't matter. If you say that René LeFlore never worked here, then she must be attempting to fool me. I'll have nothing more to do with her."

Cassie rose and put out her hand. "I'm sorry for taking up so much of your time."

"It's no trouble," said the housekeeper. "I'm happy I could be of help to you."

As the housekeeper led her to the front door, Cassie looked at her watch. The little episode in the Carnegie mansion had consumed almost a half hour. "Just about right," Cassie thought to herself.

Back in the carriage, Cassie said, "How can I ever apologize to you, Mr. Swanberg? But Mr. Carnegie is not feeling well. He has a cold and is not in any mood for chatting. He said he would be pleased, however, to meet with you another day."

Cassie's last sentence took the sting out of Swanberg's disappointment. "That's all right," he said. "One's health must come first."

As the carriage started up, there was a sudden jolt, and as Cassie lurched in her seat, her purse slipped from her lap and fell to the floor. Documents and papers spilled out of her bag.

"Oh," she gasped as she reached over to pick them up.

"Please let me do it," said Swanberg, and began gathering everything up. But the investment attorney could not help but notice the nature of the documents he was handling. On top there was a check made out to Cassandra Chadwick that was signed by Andrew Carnegie. The big bold signature awed Swanberg, but the amount of the check — five hundred thousand dollars — left him dumbfounded. There were many other securities and documents, all involving equally stupendous amounts of money.

Mr. Swanberg stuffed the papers into Cassie's bag and nervously returned it to her. The two rode on in silence for several minutes. Cassie was the first to speak. "You did see the contents of my bag, didn't you Mr. Swanberg?"

"I'm afraid I did," Swanberg said. "I just couldn't help it."

Cassie's voice was barely audible as she said, "You seem to me to be a man of great personal honor."

"Thank you, Miss Chadwick. I do pride myself on my integrity."

"Then, sir," Cassie continued, "I must ask you to call upon that integrity and never reveal what you have seen."

"I promise I never will."

Then Cassie began to weep. Drawing upon the knowledge she had gained during her months of study at the libraries of New York, she unfurled the story of her "secret" life. Swanberg listened in astonishment as Cassie began by disclosing how she had met Carnegie when he and his mother were vacationing at Skibo Castle in Scotland. She told Swanberg that she and Carnegie had fallen in love, and that their relationship had produced a child, a boy, now four years old. But Carnegie would not even consider marriage because he was so devoted to his mother.

Cassie interrupted her narrative to dab at her eyes with a handkerchief and say, "Please, I beg you, Mr. Swanberg, do not breathe a word of this to anyone."

Then she continued. "Andrew — Mr. Carnegie, I mean," she blushed, "is a gentleman. He wants to provide for me and our child. He has made certain investments for me, and he has asked me to secure an attorney — we could not use one of his attorneys, since this is so secretive — to draw up an agreement that could serve to establish my ownership of these securities."

She drew an envelope from her bag and took several slips of paper from it. "These are lists of the securities," Cassie said.

Swanberg hurriedly scanned the lists. The total amount came to more than twelve million dollars.

"Mr. Carnegie told me," Cassie continued, "that some of the securities should be deposited in a bank where they will be safe. Others should be used for trading. But I'm not sure exactly what to do. I wonder, Mr. Swanberg, whether you might be in a position to advise me."

Swanberg felt as if his dreams were coming true. To represent a client with twelve million dollars in securities could mean commissions that would increase his income tenfold. "I think I might be able to give you some assistance," he said.

"Then I should like to become one of your clients," Cassie replied.

The next time the two met, Swanberg recommended a banker who could be depended on to protect Cassie's securities. The banker's name was Duncan McDougall. A Scotsman, he was well known for his thrift and the confidential manner in which he conducted his business. Swanberg knew that the choice of McDougall would be applauded by Andrew Carnegie.

At the meeting, Cassie handed over to Swanberg a sealed envelope which she said contained seven million dollars in securities. "Please take good care of them," she urged. Then she asked Swanberg to give her a receipt for the documents. He wrote one out without hesitating. If it occurred to him to open the envelope to verify its contents, he made no move to do so. What man, after all, could doubt the word of a woman of such charm and beauty?

Cassie's plan was going even better than she had hoped it would. Another important ingredient arrived in the mail a few days later, a letter from Duncan McDougall saying that he had received the envelope containing the seven million dollars in securities from Mr. Swanberg, and that it was now resting safely in the vault of his bank.

Taking the letters from McDougall and Swanberg, Cassie went to a local bank. The bank did not hesitate a moment in allowing Cassie to borrow money. Her first loan was for a relatively small amount, only fifty thousand dollars.

When the loan fell due, Cassie paid it promptly, using a bigger loan from a second bank to obtain the money to do so. The second she paid with a third loan. And so forth. She thus established herself as a good credit risk.

In the months that followed, Cassie moved into high gear. One loan followed another in rapid succession, each greater than the preceding one. She was soon dealing in amounts that totaled many millions of dollars.

Whenever a bank seemed at all reluctant to lend her the money she asked for, Cassie called forth the names of Duncan McDougall and Casper Swanberg. They were happy to endorse Cassie's loans. And why not? They were holding seven million dollars in securities of hers — or thought they were.

Much of the money that Cassie derived from her heavy borrowing she used to purchase stocks and bonds. These she hoped would increase in value. She then planned to sell the securities, using the profits to repay her loans. A portion of the money she would keep for herself, of course.

Not all of Cassie's purchases were made at the stock market. She traveled throughout the country, staying at the finest hotels, dining at the best restaurants. She treated herself to the expensive jewelry and the best dresses that money could buy.

For a time, all went well. Whenever a bank pressed her to repay a loan, she would borrow from another bank or order Swanberg to sell some of her stock holdings. She was able to operate in this fashion for months.

What triggered Cassie's downfall was a sudden decline in stock market prices. As the value of her securities dwindled, Cassie found it harder and harder to repay her loans.

She remained cool, however. When bankers

wrote her angry letters demanding payment and hinting at legal action, Cassie simply handed them over to Swanberg and McDougall. At first, they were gentle with her, asking only that she be more careful in the manner in which she was conducting her financial manipulations.

But, eventually, the day came when McDougall called for the envelope that he believed contained the seven million dollars in securities. He was horrified to find it was filled with strips of newspaper, many of which gave evidence of Cassie's grim sense of humor in that they bore pictures of Andrew Carnegie and contained accounts of his activities.

Swanberg was beside himself with anger when he learned that he had been tricked. He didn't realize the extent of the hoax until he went to Andrew Carnegie's lawyers and told them the story.

Within a few days, Swanberg received a letter saying that Mr. Carnegie had never met the "lady" known as Constance Cassandra Chadwick, and had never in his life had anything to do with any woman bearing that name. Swanberg was crushed. He realized he had been a victim of Cassie's masquerade right from the beginning.

The police were called in. Cassie was arrested. During the trial it developed that she had borrowed more than fifty million dollars from assorted banks along the eastern seaboard of the United States. Slightly less than half of that amount had been repaid. The rest Cassie had squandered.

Cassie had no defense. Nor did she offer any apologies, either. During her trial, she described her life as an impostor as "a dream come true," saying, "I wish the dream had never ended. If I had the opportunity, I would live that dream again. It was so wonderful!"

Cassie was found guilty of fraud and sentenced to eight years in the state penitentiary. Prison life was hard on her. Her beauty quickly faded. Before she had served a fourth of her sentence, she looked as if she had aged a dozen years.

One evening, dressed in her drab prison uniform, she stretched out on the small cot in her cell, turned toward the stone wall, and fell asleep. When the jailer entered her cell the next morning, he could not wake her. Cassie had died in her sleep.

Chapter 9

Electronic Trickery

Professor Reginald Jones, a leading British government scientist during the 1940s, was a practical joker. He enjoyed pretending he was someone else and persuading friends and fellow scientists to do odd things by talking to them on the telephone.

What Jones did to Robert Tippett is an example.

He called Tippett on the telephone one afternoon. When Tippett picked up the telephone, Jones hung up.

Throughout the afternoon and into the evening, Jones repeated the sequence. He dialed Tippett's number. After a few rings, Tippett would answer. Then Jones would hang up.

Later in the evening, Jones called Tippett again, disguising his voice and impersonating a telephone company repairman. "Have you been having trouble with your telephone?" he asked.

"Indeed," declared Tippett. "All of my incoming calls are being disrupted."

"I'm sorry," Jones said. "We'll send someone out to your home next week to look at it."

"*Next week!*" Tippett cried. "I can't wait that long. How about doing something tomorrow?"

"I'm afraid not. We're understaffed at the moment. People are ill."

"You've *got* to do something. I can't be without my telephone for a week."

Jones paused before answering. "Well," he said "we might be able to do something from here. But you'd have to cooperate with us."

"I'd be glad to," said Tippett. "Just tell me what you want me to do."

"Well, first get a pencil, and tap the telephone with it. I want to hear the sound."

Tippett did as he was instructed.

"That's right," said Jones. "Can't tell yet. Keep it up."

After several more seconds of tapping, Jones said, "We're not getting a clear enough signal. What kind of shoes are you wearing? Rubber heels? I thought so. You'll have to take your shoes off. I hope you don't mind."

Tippett was happy to do so. Jones continued to lead poor Tippett through a series of such acts, with Tippett always cooperating to the fullest.

"I'm afraid we still can't tell what's wrong," Jones said. "There is one more test that we can do, but I think we'd better postpone it until the repairman can come."

"Oh, no," said Tippett. "If it's possible for me to do it, I'd like to try."

"Well, all right. There's a test that comes close to doing what we do with our own equipment. Can you get a bucket of water?"

Tippett went and got the water.

"Lower the telephone into it slowly," Jones instructed.

So it was that an intelligent and highly regarded British scientist would stand in his stocking feet in the living room of his home and dutifully dip his telephone in a bucket of water. Jones doubled up in laughter when playing such pranks.

Jones gave much thought as to why his victims behaved as they did. He delivered lectures and wrote papers on the subject. "The object," he said, "is to build up in the victim's mind a false word picture . . . so he takes action on it with confidence."

During World War II, Jones put his knowledge of hoaxing and imposture to work using the Nazi war machine as his target. The success of his efforts saved many thousands of lives and staved off the devastation of many millions of dollars in military equipment and supplies.

A tall, burly man, with pale blue eyes and rosy cheeks, Jones was assigned to the British Air Ministry during the war. He worked on radar, electronic navigation, and other scientific aspects of air warfare.

His love for practical jokes persisted. One day a high government official visited Jones and his fellow scientists at their offices in Farnborough, about thirty miles outside of London. The government official annoyed the scientists by telling them how they should be performing their duties, spelling out instructions down to the tiniest detail.

When the official returned the next day, Jones poured a bagful of soot into his umbrella. Then Jones and his collegaues prayed for rain.

Jones turned to much more serious matters in 1940, when the Battle of Britain was raging. Night after night, German bombers pummeled English cities.

Jones figured out that the night bombers were being guided to their targets by a pair of radio directional beams from the Continent. A bombing plane would fly along one beam until the pilot heard the signal from a second beam that crossed the first. He then knew his plane was over its target, and released the bombs.

Jones reported his findings to Frederick Lindemann, scientific adviser to Winston Churchill during World War II. After Lindemann told Churchill of his theory, Jones was called upon to present his views to Churchill and the nation's military leaders.

Jones spoke quietly and confidently for twenty minutes. He was able to convince Churchill that his theory was at least worth further investigation. Churchill ordered airplanes with detection equipment to be sent aloft to see whether the location of the beams could be pinpointed.

But Air Force officials rejected Jones's theory. They said that the curvature of the earth prevented radio beams from being projected long distances to be used in the manner Jones had suggested. Because of the curving, the beams simply veered off into space, they said. "It would be a waste of time to send a plane up to look for any such beams," declared one of the Air Force officers.

Jones was angered. "I know who ordered those planes up," he said. "It was Churchill himself. If the order is canceled, I'll tell him so."

No one would ever even *think* of angering Sir Winston. The planes went up, and they found the beams precisely as Jones had said they would be found.

Now the fun began. The Air Force wanted to jam the radio frequencies that were transmitting the beam signals so the German pilots could not hear them. Jones had a better idea. "Let's use the signals to misdirect the German pilots," he said. "We'll duplicate the second of the two beams. The pilots will think they're listening to their own signals, and go off course.

September and October were critical months in the Battle of Britain. But during those two months, German bombing planes were frequently led astray by British radio-beam transmissions, and the aircraft ended up dropping their bombs many miles from their intended targets.

At the time, London was a frequent target for German bombers. An Air Force officer who lived in London with his wife and three children sent his family to the country. They lived with friends many miles from any city or town. One night they were awakened by a series of heavy explosions. They looked out the window to see German planes dropping bombs in an empty field about a half a mile away. The next morning they counted more than one hundred bomb craters. They wondered what the German planes could possibly have been aiming at.

Of course, no one knew what had really happened, that the German planes had been led off course by the false radio beam. That was a deep secret, and would not be revealed to British public until after the war.

Eventually, the Germans came to realize what Jones and his colleagues were doing, and they developed another type of beam. But Jones learned how to mislead the Germans using the new beam as well. The "Battle of the Beams," as it was called, played an important part in turning the tide of the war in the Allies' favor.

The basic idea behind the beam deception was the same as when Jones had played the telephone joke on Robert Tippett. He simply controlled the channel of communication to the victim, then used it to give a false picture of the situation. Later, Jones became involved in another incident of the same type.

The British were experimenting with a device called the *G* beam, a system of radar navigation that was meant to guide British bombers to their targets in Germany and back. The experiments were in their final stages when a bomber carrying *G* beam equipment was shot down over Germany.

British Air Force officials were in a state of shock. Now the Germans knew of one of their critical secrets. It would be easy for the enemy to develop equipment to counteract the *G* beam.

The Air Force officials went to Professor Jones with their problem. They wanted to know whether they could deceive the Germans into believing the *G* beam was some other type of secret weapon.

A smile crossed Jones's face. He rubbed his hands together in anticipation. "Imagine being told to play a joke for your country," he said. "And then being given unlimited amounts of money and all the other resources that you need to do it."

Jones decided that he must make the Germans believe that the *G* beam was of no value to the British Air Force, that it was merely an experimental system. To do this, he began by developing a fake navigation system. It was a carbon copy of the twin-beam system that the Germans had been using to bomb England. Jones figured that Germans would be flattered by the fact that the British had copied them, and this would make them more willing to accept the deception. He called the new system the *J* beam.

Jones ordered the construction of three *J* beam stations in southern England. They soon began transmitting radio signals over Germany.

Jones did more. He went to British intelligence experts and asked to be put in contact with a double agent, a German spy who was actually working for the British.

Jones made up a conversation between two fake Air Force pilots that was supposedly overheard at the Ritz Bar in London. In their conversation, the pilots talked about the *J* beam, praising it highly. The double agent included the conversation in a report he was feeding back to Germany.

The Germans were completely fooled by the hoax. They forgot all about the *G* beam. Only the *J* beam concerned them, and they started jamming all *J* beam transmissions. All the while, British bombers were using *G* beam radar signals to find their targets in Germany.

After about six months, the Germans caught on to what was happening. They started jamming the radar.

Jones knew what to do. He advised Air Force officials to start using the *J* beam system for guidance. The Germans, believing the *J* beam was a hoax, had stopped jamming it.

About a year later, a similar incident occurred involving the H2S, a secret target-seeking device that worked by short-wave radio. Planted in the nose of a bomb or an artillery shell, it could guide the weapon right to its target. While an H2S unit was being tested, the plane carrying it crashed in Holland. The Germans were able to capture the equipment almost intact.

When handed the problem, Jones sought to make the Germans believe that the H2S equipment was something that it wasn't. Again using a double agent, he fed back to Germany the information that the H2S was actually an infra-red detection device that was intended to seek out submarines.

He even had a photographic expert produce an infra-red picture of a submarine taken from the air. He made sure that the picture fell into enemy hands.

Jones's hoax was more successful than he ever dreamed it would be. In an effort to prevent the British from using the infra-red equipment to detect submarines, the Germans developed an infra-red paint. It was manufactured from crushed glass, black paint pigments, and several other ingredients. Once applied to the hull of a submarine, the sub could not be distinguished from the surrounding water by an infra-red detector.

Jones was amazed. The Germans had developed a solution for a problem that didn't even exist. It was like someone taking medicine for a sickness before getting sick.

Meanwhile, the British were using their H2S equipment without German interference. Many months went by before the Germans came to realize that the H2S was for target-seeking, and had nothing to do with infra-red detection.

After the war, Jones was made a Companion of the British Empire for the services he had rendered. The American government awarded him the Legion of Merit for what he had done by helping the U.S. Navy in locating German radar stations along the coast of France in the weeks before D-Day.

He joined Aberdeen University in Scotland as a Professor of Physics, and remained there until Winston Churchill became Prime Minister again in 1951. Churchill asked Jones to join him in the government, working in scientific intelligence, and Jones did. He also held a high government post from 1962 to 1963. He then returned to Aberdeen University.

Unlike many scientists who worked with the armed services during the war, Jones admired the military men and enjoyed their company. He was a frequent guest at the reunions of their squadrons and regiments. Both of his daughters married Army officers.

Someone once asked Professor Jones whether he actually enjoyed the war. He admitted that he liked the sense of urgency that prevailed during the war years. " 'It was more important to be right than to be polite,' " said Jones, quoting Winston Churchill.

"And there was the feeling of power," Jones said. "You made a decision and things really got done."

But the hoaxing and deception were what he enjoyed more than anything else. "After all," he said, "It was something I had been preparing for for years."

Chapter 10

The Skywayman

Young Frank Abagnale had what he described as a bumblebee personality. He was always flying where he wasn't supposed to fly, making a pot of honey on the side.

During the late 1960s and early 1970s, Abagnale was one of the most hunted impostors and fraudulent check writers in the history of crime. Masquerading as an airline pilot, lawyer, doctor, and college professor, Abagnale led American law enforcement officials and the police of several foreign countries on a long and frustrating chase before he was finally arrested and sent to prison.

"Money was only part of it," said Abagnale, who was known as "The Skywayman." "I had fun fooling people. It was exciting and at times glamorous. But I was always aware that if and when I was caught, I wasn't going to win any Oscars. I was going to prison."

Frank Abagnale was born in Bronxville, New York, a well-to-do suburb just north of New York

City. His parents separated when he was twelve, and Frank went to live with his father.

Mr. Abagnale owned a big stationery store in New York and it took up most of his time. Frank was seldom disciplined. Instead of going to school, he teamed up with young boys from his neighborhood, and the gang would spend the day shoplifting or trying to slip into a movie theater without paying.

Frank was more mature than his companions, and much bigger. By the time he was fifteen, he was six feet tall and weighed 170 pounds. When he and his friends were together, Frank looked like a schoolteacher who was taking his students on a field trip.

Frank's father bought him a car, which became the second most important thing in his life. Girls were the first. He spent about every waking hour in pursuit of them.

Mr. Abagnale allowed Frank to use his credit card to buy gasoline for the car. It was agreed, however, that when the bill arrived at the end of the month, Frank was to pay it, using money he earned at a part-time job as a shipping clerk.

The arrangement worked well for a month. When the end of the month arrived and Frank had to pay the gasoline bill, he had no money left. Not having money hampered him in his pursuit of young women.

One day when he was passing a gasoline station, Frank noticed a sign that advertised tires. An idea struck him. He pulled into the station and priced a set of new whitewalls. "For this car, they'd come to one hundred sixty dollars," the owner told him.

Frank nodded, then presented the station-owner a proposition. "I really don't need any tires," he said. "What I need is money. Here's what I'd like to do: I'll buy a set of tires and pay for them with this credit card. But I'm not going to take the tires. You just give me one hundred dollars instead."

The station-owner thought for a minute. He realized that when the bill for the tires was paid, he'd get back his one hundred dollars. But he'd still have the tires. Then when he *really* sold them, he'd get another one hundred sixty dollars. The station-owner agreed to go along with the scheme. Frank rolled out of the station with one hundred dollars in his pocket and a big grin on his face.

After a week of high living, Frank tried the hoax again. It worked again. He tried it so many times in the next few weeks that he lost count. Not only did he "buy" tires, but he'd sign for batteries, other accessories, and extra gallons of gasoline that never went into his tank.

When the bills for his purchases began arriving at the Abagnale home, Frank would intercept them before they reached his father, and toss them into the wastebasket. He knew he was simply postponing a showdown, but he was having so much fun he didn't worry about it.

One day an investigator from the oil company's credit bureau sought out Mr. Abagnale at his store. He wanted to know two things. When was the company going to get paid? And why was it necessary to purchase thirty-four hundred dollars in gas, tires, batteries, and other supplies in the space of two months? "The car you're driving must be a real lemon," the investigator said. "You ought to think about trading it in."

Mr. Abagnale was shocked. He demanded to see the charge receipts. Each bore Frank's signature.

That night Mr. Abagnale confronted his son. "Why did you do it?" he wanted to know. Frank shook his head in bewilderment. "It's the girls, dad," he said. "It's the girls."

Frank's father forgave him and paid the bill. He did not punish his son.

Not long after, Mr. Abagnale was struck with a series of misfortunes; he lost his business and was forced to take a job at the local post office. There were drastic changes in life at the Abagnale home. Instead of driving a Cadillac, Mr. Abagnale now had to get around in a beat-up Chevy. Instead of wearing hand-tailored suits, he dressed in his letter carrier's uniform.

Mr. Abagnale never complained. But the situation depressed Frank. He didn't like seeing what was happening to his father.

One morning, Frank woke up and decided he would run away. He had not made any plans to do so. He just felt that it was time for him to go.

He didn't travel far, only a few miles south to New York City. As a sixteen-year-old high school dropout, Frank quickly found that his services were not in great demand. The best job he could get was as a stockboy in a stationery store. It paid only sixty dollars a week. Frank had to live in a seedy hotel, eat at cafeterias, or buy food from sidewalk vendors. Worst of all, he couldn't afford to date any girls.

Frank believed the reason he was so poorly paid was that he was so young. Since he already had the appearance of a much older person, he decided he would make other people believe he *was* older. He did so by altering the date of his birth as it appeared on his driver's license, changing it from 1948 to 1938. Now when he went to see a prospective employer, he could proclaim he was twenty-six.

This improved his income, but not a great deal. Frank was able to get a job as a truck driver's helper at a salary of one hundred ten dollars a week. He then came to the conclusion that it was not his lack of years that was limiting his income but his lack of education. Employers simply would not pay top-flight wages to a high school dropout.

When Frank had left home, his assets included a checking account which contained two hundred dollars. Whenever he was in need of money, he would write a check on his account. The checks were not large, usually only ten or twenty dollars. He cashed them at one of the bank's local branches. Frank soon learned he could also cash his checks at department stores, hotels, or neighborhood supermarkets. All he had to do was show his driver's license as identification.

One day as he was writing out a check, Frank realized that he must have about used up the two hundred dollars in his account. But the fact that he was overdrawn didn't stop him from cashing the check. No one at the store asked him any questions. They just handed over the money.

In the weeks that followed, Frank continued to pass bad checks whenever he needed money.

When he found that he could support himself with the worthless checks, he quit his job.

Frank now realized that he was a crook, but it didn't bother him. He had no desire to give up his career. What did make him feel uncomfortable was the thought that the police were undoubtedly looking for him. A stiff prison term loomed in his future. He decided he would have to leave New York to avoid arrest and imprisonment. But if he fled to another state, he realized his New York driver's license would no longer be of any value to him as a piece of identification. He would have to establish a new identity.

One day as he was puzzling over his clouded future, he happened to be passing a midtown Manhattan hotel when an airline flight crew consisting of a pilot, co-pilot, flight engineer, and several stewardesses emerged. They were all laughing and joking, obviously having a good time. Frank watched them as they entered a limousine which would take them to one of the airfields serving New York.

Slowly an idea began taking shape in Frank's mind. What if he were to become an airline pilot? He was not considering becoming a real pilot, of course, not someone who controlled a giant airliner, but instead, an individual who garbed himself in a pilot's uniform and carried pilot's identification.

There were countless advantages to playing such a role. Airline pilots were men who were respected and trusted. An airline pilot could walk into any bank, hotel, department store, or other business and, with proper identification, cash a check instantly.

The more Frank thought about it, the more the idea of becoming a phony airline pilot appealed to him. His first task was to obtain a pilot's uniform. He called the main switchboard at Pan Am headquarters in New York and asked for the purchasing department. Frank told the man who answered the telephone that he was a Pan Am pilot based in Los Angeles. "Someone's stolen my uniform." he said, "and I've got a flight out tonight. Where can I get a replacement uniform in a hurry?"

"No problem," the man said, and he gave Frank the name and address of a uniform company in New York. "Go down there," the man instructed. "Tell Mr. Rosen to fit you up. I'll tell him you're coming. What's your name again?" Frank gave the man a phony name.

Not long after, Frank walked into the uniform company and asked for Mr. Rosen, who provided him with an airline pilot's jacket, trousers, tie, and visored cap. Frank signed an invoice which was to be sent to Pan Am for payment.

Before he left the store, Frank checked his appearance in the mirror. He noticed immediately something was missing—the Pan Am emblem worn on the uniform jacket and cap.

He asked Rosen for them. The uniform manufacturer gave Frank a puzzled look. "We don't carry emblems," he said. "That's hardware. You get hardware from the company, from the stores department."

"Oh, right," said Frank, flashing a grin.

When he got back to his room, Frank telephoned Pan Am headquarters again. "I wonder whether you could help me," he said. "I have to make a delivery to your stores department. Where is it located, please?"

"Hangar 14, Kennedy Airport," the switch-board operator said.

An hour later, Frank was standing outside Hangar 14. An enormous structure, almost a hundred feet in height, it seemed capable of housing the largest aircraft in Pan Am's jet fleet. The hangar was enclosed by a tall, sturdy chain-link fence which was topped with several strands of barbed wire. Armed guards were posted at the hangar entrances.

Frank noticed that when a pilot, stewardess, or other uniformed employee entered the hangar area, he or she would parade through the gate without being stopped. Then Frank saw why they were able to gain admittance so easily. Each of the pilots wore an ID card. It was clipped to the breast pocket of their uniforms. The stewardesses had ID cards, too, which they pinned to their purse straps.

Frank's plans were sidetracked, but not for long. Since rain had been threatened that day, he had purchased a black raincoat similar to the ones he had seen pilots wearing. He had also brought along his newly acquired uniform in a small suitcase.

Frank went into one of the airport bathrooms and changed into the uniform. Then he walked to the main entrance of Hangar 14. As he approached the gate, he took the raincoat and tossed it over his left shoulder, adjusting it so it covered the left side of his jacket, the side on which he would have worn his ID card, if he had owned one. He waltzed confidently through the gate.

When the guard turned toward him, Frank gave him a friendly wave. "Good afternoon," he said with a smile. The guard murmured a greeting. He made no effort to stop Frank.

Once inside the hangar, Frank checked a wall directory to find out the location of the stores department. "Can I help you?" the clerk said when Frank entered, the raincoat still draped over his left shoulder. "I need a jacket and hat emblem," Frank said. "My youngster took mine and lost them."

The clerk nodded, then disappeared among the long rows of shelves. When he returned, he slid the two emblems across the counter to Frank, who immediately pinned one to his hat, the other to his jacket.

"Give me your name and employee number," the clerk said, taking a form behind the counter. "Name's Robert Black," Frank said, "Number 35099."

When Frank left the store, he wandered about the hangar building for a time, mingling with the Pan Am employees. He no longer felt like an unemployed sixteen-year-old. But he didn't quite feel like a Pan Am pilot, either. He lacked an ID card. He knew his deception could never be successful without one.

When he returned to his Manhattan hotel room, Frank set to work obtaining a card. In the Yellow Pages of the New York telephone directory, Frank found the name of several firms that manufactured ID cards. He picked one out and, switching to a business suit, paid the company a visit.

"I'm Frank Williams of Carib Airlines," he

106

told one of the company's sales representatives. "We've just started operations here in the United States. We're using temporary ID cards for our employees right now, but we plan to issue cards enclosed in plastic to each of them. You know," Frank continued, "the kind of card that other airlines use. Can you show me some samples, please?"

The salesman was happy to help. He showed Frank dozens of different types of cards. "This is the one most of the airlines use," he said. Frank picked up the card and examined it carefully. It seemed to be very similar to the Pan Am ID card, except that it lacked the company name and trademark.

"This looks like the card we want," Frank said. "I'd like to take it to show to my boss."

"By all means," said the salesman. He tucked the card into an envelope along with a price list and handed it to Frank.

That night Frank filled in the card. He chose to identify himself as "Frank Williams." He typed in the name, position, and employee number. He arranged to have his photograph taken and mounted in the space provided.

Frank was wondering how he was going to obtain the Pan Am name in its distinctive lettering and the company trademark when he happened to pass a hobby shop. There in the window were displayed models of commercial jet aircraft. One of them was a Pan Am 707. The model bore the Pan Am trademark and, on the wings and fuselage, the company's name.

Frank purchased one of the models and brought it to his room. He threw away the parts. Following the instructions, he soaked the decals in warm water, then transferred the designs he wanted to the ID card. When the decals dried, they looked as if they had been printed on the card. The last step was to get the card laminated between two thin layers of plastic.

When the card was finished, Frank bought a holder, and clipped it to his breast pocket. Now he felt like a real fake pilot.

But Frank realized that he needed more than a uniform and an ID card to be a successful impostor. He also needed a great deal of information about the profession of airline pilot. He started visiting libraries and reading all he could about commercial aviation. He read every flying magazine he could lay his hands on. He began to visit flight-crew lounges at the airports near New York City. There he would chat with pilots, flight engineers, and stewardesses about their airlines, the different types of equipment they flew, and the routes with which they were familiar.

It was almost like learning a foreign language. One thing that helped Frank was a notebook he kept. In it he jotted down all the miscellaneous pieces of information that he learned and which every pilot should know. For example, he learned it was standard procedure for eastbound planes to fly at odd-numbered altitudes (17,000 feet, 25,000 feet, etc.), while westbound flights flew at even-numbered levels (18,000 feet, 22,000 feet, etc.). He learned the abbreviations the airline industry used for various cities and airports: CLE was Cleveland, NWK, Newark, and LOA, Los Angeles.

Into the notebook went scores of new words

and their definitions, including aileron (a movable portion of the plane's wing), glide scope (a runway approach light used in guiding a plane in for a landing), and taxiway (an area between a terminal and the landing or takeoff strip over which planes move). He also entered the names of every flight-crew member he met.

Frank loved wearing his uniform and being taken for an airline pilot. Men gave him admiring glances. Pretty women smiled at him. Pilots and stewardesses would always nod or utter some words of greeting as they passed. The uniform gave him approval and respect. He had never experienced anything like it.

During the time he was gathering information about airline operations and personnel, one of the terms that Frank encountered was "deadheading." It referred to the privilege that flight-crew members enjoy that enables them to travel free. For example, if a Pan Am pilot not on duty wanted to fly from New York to Los Angeles, he could travel on American Airlines, United, TWA, or any other carrier serving the city, and not be charged.

Frank had not been involved in his masquerade for very long when he decided he would take a flight as a deadhead. He took an airport limousine to LaGuardia Airport and went to the office of Eastern Airlines. "I want to deadhead on your next flight to Miami," he told a clerk there. At the same time, Frank produced his phony ID card and showed it to the man.

"We've got a flight going in twenty minutes," the man said. "Do you want to catch that?"

"That'll be great," Frank said. The clerk gave

Frank a form to fill out. It required his name, employee number, the position he held with Pan Am, and his destination. After Frank had completed the form, the man took it, tore off a carbon copy, and handed it to Frank. "Give this to the stewardess as you board," he said.

"The jump seat is open, if you want it," the man added. Frank knew the jump seat was a small folding seat in the cockpit. It was often used by federal aviation officials, top-level airline personnel, or deadheading pilots. Frank agreed to take the jump seat.

Frank boarded the plane and entered the cockpit. The pilot, first officer, and flight engineer were busy with their pre-flight routine of checking various aircraft systems, and merely nodded in his direction. Frank didn't know what the jump seat looked like. He was relieved when the flight engineer closed the cabin door and indicated the tiny seat mounted on the door's inside panel.

No one spoke to Frank until the plane was airborne and had reached cruising altitude. Then the crew members began to chat with him. "How long have you been with Pan Am?" the pilot asked. "What kind of equipment do you fly?" he wanted to know. "Were you in the service?" the first officer asked. When Frank answered no, the first officer asked Frank where he had received his pilot training. Frank had ready answers for all the questions. He felt the flight crew had hardly tested him.

The next day, Frank deadheaded to Dallas, and from there, to San Francisco. During the next two years, Frank traveled to every part of the United

States and through much of Europe—and always as a deadhead.

Deadheading was not the most serious of frauds that Frank committed. Using the name Frank Williams, the name that appeared on his pilot's ID card, Frank opened a checking account in New York. By so doing, he received two hundred checks, each bearing his name and the post office box number he had given the bank as his address. Cashing the checks was child's play. The first checks he cashed were good, but hundreds of others that he wrote in the months that followed had all the value of Monopoly money.

At first, Frank did not write large checks, limiting their amounts to fifty or seventy-five dollars. Most of these were cashed at airline ticket counters, hotels, and motels. Sometimes clerks wouldn't even ask for identification.

Frank didn't operate in the same city for too long a period. After a week or two in Chicago, for instance, he would deadhead to San Francisco, booking a room in a local hotel or motel where real flight crews stayed. Or sometimes he'd rent an apartment in the city where he planned to set up operations. Once he had established an address for himself, Frank would open a personalized checking account. When his checks arrived in the mail, he'd go on a check-writing spree.

All of this took place in the early to mid-1960s. It's not likely that Frank would have been as successful in passing fraudulent checks today as he was then. The National Crime Information Center, a federally sponsored agency which is now in operation, links the nation's police departments

111

by computer with an enormous pool of information about criminals and their activities. In Frank's case, local police seldom had any idea they were dealing with a professional impostor and check forger.

And airport security in general was not as strict as it is today. Frank operated in a time before the great wave of aircraft hijackings and terrorist bombings. When these began to occur, airlines and airline terminals began to take greater precautions against sabotage and theft.

Another thing that always worked in Frank's favor was the image people have of the American airline pilot. As an apparent pilot, Frank was trusted and respected. Airline personnel at ticket counters and hotel clerks took his checks and cashed them, and were happy and eager to do so.

Yet Frank fully realized he was being hunted. Occasionally he'd get a case of the jitters, believing that one law enforcement agency or another was closing in on him. When that happened, he'd stop writing checks and hole up for a time. Frank couldn't be blamed for getting nervous. After all, he was only seventeen.

After two years of posing as an airline pilot, Frank experienced his first serious brush with the law. While deadheading on a flight from New Orleans to Miami, Frank's status as a pilot was seriously questioned. The numbers that appeared on Frank's ID card and his forged pilot's license were radioed ahead to Miami, and police were on hand to meet the plane when it landed there. They took Frank into custody. The FBI was called in and Frank was questioned. It happened to be the weekend, however, and the Pan Am offices in New York were closed. It was thus impossible to check Frank's story against company employment records. Authorites in Miami had no choice but to release him.

It was a scary experience for Frank. He decided he would abandon his masquerade as an airline pilot, at least temporarily. For reasons he never quite understood, Frank had always felt safe and secure in the city of Atlanta. He rented an apartment there, posing as Frank Williams, a pediatrician, that is, a physician who specializes in the treatment of young children. Before deserting Atlanta, eighteen-year-old "Dr. Frank Williams" had become a pediatrics consultant at a local hospital.

Frank's next escapade took him to Baton Rouge, Louisiana. There he learned that the state attorney general was seeking assistants for his staff. With forged documents proclaiming that he was a graduate of Harvard Law School, and four months of diligent study, Frank became a Louisiana lawyer. It took him three tries, however, before he passed the state examination that served to make his status official. Then a real Harvard lawyer appeared upon the scene. Frank decided it was time to move on once again.

After touring the West for several weeks, Frank landed a position as a professor of sociology at Brigham Young University in Provo, Utah. Forged credentials testifying that he held a college degree from Columbia University convinced Brigham Young officials that he had the necessary educational background. Frank also fabricated letters of recommendation from officials of City

College of New York. Frank's "secret" in becoming a successful college professor was simply to teach by the book and keep one chapter ahead of the students.

In the years that followed, Frank resumed his role as Frank Williams, Pan Am pilot, but moved operations to Europe. In Paris, where he spent much of his time, he tricked a printer into making up several thousand checks bearing the Pan Am name and trademark. He not only cashed the checks throughout France but went back to the United States for a brief check-writing binge.

Before he returned to France, Frank was apprehended and jailed, but once again he was able to talk his way to freedom. The incident later helped him to make up his mind to put aside his criminal activities and retire. He had not yet reached his twenty-first birthday.

Frank abandoned the role of Frank Williams, airline pilot, and became Roger Monjo, an author and screenwriter. He bought a modest home in the small village of Montpellier in the south of France, about one hundred miles to the west of Marseilles. Since he spoke French, it was not difficult for Abagnale to make friends and adapt to his surroundings.

Although Montpellier was not served by any major airline, the town was often visited by vacationing flight-crew members. One day, an Air France stewardess who had once dated Frank spotted him in a local market. When the stewardess returned to Paris, she told Air France officials that she had seen Frank Williams. The police were called.

Not long after, Frank was shopping at the same

market where he had been recognized, when a horde of French detectives and security agents descended upon him. At the Montpellier police station, Frank was made to admit his real identity. A trial quickly followed. Frank was found guilty of fraud and sentenced to a year in prison.

Frank was not too disappointed. A year in prison was not a heavy sentence for his years of criminal activity. But the prison to which Frank was confined was a hellhole. Frank was stripped of his clothes and thrown into a cell that was only five feet on each side and five feet tall. The walls were stone; the ceiling and door were steel.

There was no light in the cell, no sink, no toilet, only a bucket. It was drafty and cold. Frank was fed three times a day. For breakfast, a guard brought him bread and water; for lunch, a watery soup and bread; and for dinner, coffee and bread. He was not once permitted to leave the cell.

When finally released from the prison, Frank was in a half-crazed state. His body was covered with infected sores. His hair was long and thickly matted.

Other European countries were eager to prosecute Frank for his illegal check-cashing activities: Sweden, Germany, Italy, Spain, Switzerland, and Denmark among them. The French police turned him over to Swedish authorities. A Swedish judge sentenced him to prison term of six months. Compared to the French prison, the Swedish jail was a country club.

Frank might have spent most of the rest of his life being shipped from one European country to another, paying for his crimes in each, but he was able to get Swedish authorities to deport him to the United States. Forgery, passing bad checks, swindling, and using the mails to defraud were some of the crimes Frank was charged with in America. When he was brought to trial, he pleaded guilty. He was sentenced to a twelve-year term in the Federal Correctional Institution in Petersburg, Virginia.

He served four years of the sentence and was then paroled. He worked in a pizza parlor and later held a job as a movie projectionist before becoming an anti-crime specialist, advising banks, hotels, airlines, and other businesses on how to protect themselves against fraud and theft. A company he formed grew by leaps and bounds. Today, Frank supervises a highly trained staff from the firm's headquarters in Houston. A book about his life, titled *Catch Me If You Can*, was published in 1980. A feature film based on the book was released not long after. Ironically, Frank's new career has provided him with all the glamour and excitement he sought in his years as an impostor.

Chapter 11

Dangerous Game

No book that at all concerns impostors would be complete without some mention of America's wartime intelligence agents, men and women who operated in enemy territory during World War II, assuming different names, characters, and professions in seeking to blend in with the native population.

These agents were perhaps the cleverest impostors of all time. They had to be. For anyone who failed to be convincing in the role he or she played, the penalty was capture and even torture and death.

At the height of World War II, there were about twelve thousand secret agents working in foreign countries for the United States. They represented the Office of Strategic Services — the OSS, the agency responsible for wartime intelligence gathering and sabotage.

Dropped by plane or landed by rubber raft, many of these agents were assigned to direct sabotage operations. They often supervised or cooperated with guerrilla units, blowing up factories, power plants, fuel storage facilities, supply trains, and bridges. They also acted to direct commando strikes, and they suggested targets for large-scale bombing missions.

They were a rather bizarre assortment of individuals. They had to have, first of all, the ability to speak and write foreign languages smoothly and easily. In order to be given an assignment in France, for example, an agent had to speak French as well as a Parisian.

Agents had to have a deep-seated knowledge of the country to which they were assigned, knowing not only the obvious facts about the country, but also the trivial information any citizen would know. If he or she was to be stationed in Paris, he would be expected to know how much a ticket cost to a local movie, or how long the train ride was from Paris to Lyon.

Consequently, many OSS agents were foreign-born Americans. Some of them were refugees from Germany or Italy. They represented a wide range of professions. There were bankers, lawyers, teachers, actors, and salesmen among them.

Not all agents were men. About fifty female agents were sent into France during World War II. Of this number, fifteen were arrested by the Gestapo, and only three of the women from this group survived.

Long months of careful preparation were necessary before an agent could be sent into the field. Each agent's clothing and the documents he was to carry had to be correct down to the tiniest detail.

The clothing and documents section of the Office of Strategic Services was located in the center of London. It was staffed by a tailor, shoe-maker, experts in printing and photoengraving, and specialists in paper and textiles.

Clothing to be worn by the agent had to be an exact copy of what was being worn on the Continent. Agents were sent to the Continent regularly to gather samples of uniforms, civilian clothing, and documents in general use. Samples of all such items were kept on file at the OSS headquarters in London, and the files were constantly being brought up to date.

In the manufacturing of a suit that a double agent was to wear, every detail was considered of vital importance. In England, it was the custom to sew on four-holed buttons by threading the holes in parallel. But this method had to be scrapped in favor of the Continental style of threading the buttons in crisscross fashion.

On the inside of the suit jacket, there had to be a pocket on both sides, not merely on the right side, as was the custom in England and the United States. Suspender buttons had to be marked "elegant," or "for gentlemen," or "mode de Paris," as was usual in both France and Germany.

The effort to make an American look like a European had its painful aspects. American agents being sent on missions into France had to have all their dental work redone in the French style. All gold caps, crowns, and fillings had to come out; silver went in.

An enormous amount of time and effort went into the preparation of false identity papers and similar documents. Every person in Europe carried an identity card. The Gestapo, the German secret police, checked identity cards constantly. Work permits and travel documents were also checked.

Because so many of their agents were sent into France, the OSS operated a special French Documents Section. The section collected samples of papers carried by French citizens, and then sought to fake them as accurately as possible. Paper, ink, and the style and size of type had to match perfectly.

At one time, the French Documents Section had a noted forger on its staff. Known as "Jim the Penman," he had been in and out of American jails throughout most of his adult life. He forged signatures on hundreds of documents for agents working in Europe. He was an absolute master in forging the signature of Heinrich Himmler, chief of the SS troops, the elite military unit of the Nazi Party.

To age documents, they were sometimes rubbed in ashes or in a powder that was made of crushed rock. Document corners were carefully rounded with sandpaper. Workers in the document section would carry documents in their hip and jacket pockets for weeks at a time until they had absorbed perspiration. An agent never went into the field without his documents being properly sweat-stained.

The French Documents Section kept an extensive file of schools, businesses, and government agencies that had been laid to waste in bombing raids. Whenever possible, an agent was given papers that showed his birthplace, residence, school, and place of employment to be in a town where all such official records had been destroyed.

The Germans were then unable to check the information that appeared on the document.

The Gestapo soon became aware that American and British agents were carrying forged documents, so they constantly made document changes in an effort to trap the agents. One of these changes involved the introduction of a different nine-digit number on all French identity cards. As soon as the French Documents Section learned of this change, they began imprinting a nine-digit number on all identity cards they turned out. But agents carrying the new card were quickly picked up by the Gestapo.

Experts in London then realized the nine-digit number was a coded number, and they immediately set to work to break the code. Eventually, they did. The code worked like this:

• The first three digits represented a city in France, with each of the French cities having been assigned a code number.

• The next five digits represented the day, month, and year of the card-bearer's birth.

• The last number indicated the bearer's sex. An even number was a male, and odd number, a female.

But breaking the code wasn't enough. The document makers also needed the secret list of French cities and the corresponding code number for each. An agent was assigned to steal a copy of the list — and did.

Once an agent was provided with proper documents and garbed in clothing that looked authentic, even to a close observer, he or she then required a cover story. Without a job or a profession, without some reason for being where he was and doing what he was doing, the agent's real identity was in constant jeopardy.

The cover story, whenever possible, was made to match the agent's personality and previous work experience or training. One agent, for instance, had great skill as a painter. Bearing the code name Aramis, he spent months roaming the streets of Paris with his easel, paints, and brushes. Often he seemed to be painting the beautiful bridges across the River Seine. What he was actually doing was making sketches of the fortifications the Germans had installed along the river banks. He was also used as a lookout by underground groups planning sabotage activities at times when they were placing blasting charges in strategic places.

One strong point in Aramis's favor was his age. He was sixty years old. A younger man would have attracted attention. "Why aren't you in the Army, like everyone else?" the Gestapo would have surely wanted to know.

A weakness in Aramis's cover story was that he never sold any of his paintings. If he had ever been questioned, he might have had a difficult time explaining the source of his money.

Other times, a cover story was fabricated from beginning to end, and then memorized by the agent. Often these stories were based on the lives of real persons, individuals who had fled to England from the Continent just before or even during the war.

Would-be agents were also given what were called Stress Interviews. The candidate would be seated on a straight-backed chair in a darkened room with a bright light shining in his or her face. Staff members would act as enemy police and take turns questioning the candidate for hour after hour without any reprieve, accusing the agent of all manner of crimes and threatening him or her with physical punishment.

No matter how the would-be agent reacted to the long, agonizing test, the candidate was always told that he or she had failed. Staff members watched closely to see how the candidate reacted to this news. If he or she broke down emotionally, release from the course quickly followed.

One agent was arrested in France because the Gestapo did not believe his cover story that he was a former prisoner of a German concentration camp. When questioned, the agent was able to give a complete and detailed description of the camp, recite the names of other prisoners, the name of the camp commander, the names of some of the guards, and even the name of the prison doctor.

But the Gestapo officers still had their doubts. They called a German soldier who had been a guard at the camp and asked him to verify the agent's story. After talking with him for a number of days, the guard said that absolutely everything the agent man said was accurate. The Gestapo released the agent, and even apologized for arresting him.

As a last resort in the face of brutal torture, and to keep from revealing secrets that they knew, agents carried what was called an *L* pill. About the size of an aspirin tablet, the *L* pill contained two poisons, potassium and cyanide. If placed in the mouth and chewed, the pill caused death in a matter of minutes.

But the L pill was coated with a substance that would not dissolve in the mouth or even in the stomach. The idea was, when captured, to pop the L pill into one's mouth. If not tortured, the agent simply swallowed the pill without chewing it.

Agents were supplied with special containers for storing secret messages or an L pill. A male agent might carry a razor, the handle of which was hollow. It looked exactly like the standard razor one might purchase at a supermarket.

Cigarette lighters were also used for concealing messages. The body of the lighter would be a hollow shell, opened by a secret lever. But intelligence agents had to give up using lighters because the German police, not knowing their secret use, took the lighters for themselves. The agent not only lost the lighter, but any message it might have contained.

Female agents often made use of a message-carrying lipstick tube. The lipstick would be melted, the message tube inserted in the metal container, and the lipstick would be cast around the tube in its original shape.

Buttons on clothing were a favorite hiding place. A button would be sliced in two, and then the top and base hollowed out. The two halves would then be threaded so they could be screwed together.

The Germans found out about the button trick. Intelligence officers were about to abandon the use of buttons when someone suggested reversing the direction of the threads. To unscrew a container, it is normal to twist or turn the top or lid to the left. The button-containers worked in that manner. But with the threads reversed, twisting or turning to the left only served to tighten the top half. This simple change was enough to deceive the Germans.

Agents were given training in many different fields. One five-week course included instruction in a variety of weapons, in judo and other forms of unarmed combat, demolition, the use of small boats, and wireless operation.

The last named was especially important. Before an agent was sent into the field, he had to operate a secret radio from a location in England, sending coded messages to his instructor.

Instructors came to know each student's "fist" — the particular style that characterized the messages the agent transmitted. A person's fist is just as distinctive as his or her handwriting.

Sometimes this knowledge proved very valuable. When messages for an agent who was code-named Lion Tamer resumed after two weeks of silence, his former instructor was called in to receive the transmissions. The instructor could tell at once that it was not the former student who was sending. The officials realized the Germans had captured Lion Tamer and his codebook, and were transmitting in his name.

Agents were also trained in parachute jumping. The course lasted only one week, a very brief period of time, considering American paratroopers spent many weeks merely preparing for their first jump. In that week, each agent made four practice jumps—three by day, one at night.

After their training in parachute jumping, each

agent was given a final examination that took the form of a four-day field trial. Each man or woman was placed in a situation similar to one he or she might encounter when operating in enemy territory. Instructors judged how well they reacted to various problems they were made to face, and whether they were able to put to use what they learned in their training sessions.

Most students were then given additional instruction at one of several specialized schools. Some became experts in demolition; others, in industrial sabotage. Still others went on to pilot training, in the use of aircraft in picking up and delivering agents in hostile country.

E. F. Floege was the first special agent to parachute into France. A 45-year-old native of Chicago, Floege had lived in France for many years before the war, and had operated a bus company in the town of Angers, about 150 miles southeast of Paris.

Floege was to pose as a farmer. The French underground had arranged for a farmhouse in which he was to live in the village of Mee, about twenty miles from Angers. Floege would thus be operating in an area he knew very well.

Floege was dropped near the city of Tours, met by a member of the underground, and taken to Mee. He began organizing a group of saboteurs almost immediately. He kept in contact with headquarters in London by radio and was assigned his own radio operator. Floege also worked through two couriers, one of whom was his son, who still lived in France.

In the fall of 1943, Floege and his colleagues received seven drops of arms and supplies. The group was about ready to perform their first act of sabotage when Floege's son was picked up by the Gestapo.

During their period of training, agents were instructed in how to cope when undergoing hard questioning by the enemy. It was explained that even the toughest of men would eventually break under torture. But every agent was instructed not to reveal any secret information for a period of forty-eight hours after capture. This would give other members of their group time to flee the area.

But Floege's son had no training as an agent. He broke down quickly under Gestapo interrogation, and disclosed the names and addresses of the men and women in Floege's group. One by one, the Gestapo began tracking them down.

André Bouchardon, Floege's wireless operator, was trapped in a restaurant in Mee by seven Gestapo men. As they tried to handcuff him, Bouchardon kicked one man in the groin. The man whipped out his pistol and shot Bouchardon in the chest. He fell to the floor, pretending to be dead. Three of the Gestapo agents picked up Bouchardon's body and thrust it into the back seat of their car.

Two Gestapo men rode in the front seat, while one stayed in the back with Bouchardon's "corpse." But Bouchardon was far from dead; he wasn't even unconscious. He managed to slip his hand into his jacket pocket, draw out his revolver, and shoot the man next to him and the two agents in front. The car spun out of control and crashed into a ditch. Bourchardon crawled out of the wreckage and made his way to a nearby farmhouse where friends lived.

Floege, meanwhile, was unaware that his son had been arrested and that the Gestapo was picking up his companions. He was working on his farm when he saw a car pull into the driveway. Three men got out, drew guns, and began to approach him. Floege raced for a high wall at the edge of his property, scrambled over it, and fled to the same house where Bouchardon was hiding.

Together, Floege and Bouchardon went to Paris. There they waited until they could be passed on to other members of the underground who smuggled them into Spain. From Spain, they returned to England.

In the spring of 1944, Floege and Bouchardon were dropped into France again. This time their efforts were much more successful.

They were assigned to take over a guerrilla group with the code name Stockbroker. Although there was a shortage of explosives at the time, Stockbroker still managed to destroy factories, railroads, and power stations.

Floege learned that the Peugeot works was making tank turrets and other tank parts for the Germans. He met with Peugeot officials and asked them to cooperate with the saboteurs. If they did not, Floege told them, he would call in Allied bombers, and the entire Peugeot plant would be leveled. The officials decided to cooperate, permitting plant machinery to be wrecked, which crippled the output of tank parts.

One day, Floege and Bouchardon developed a new and inexpensive method of sabotage. They stopped a freight train about two miles before it reached its destination. After persuading the engineer and his assistants to leave, they got up steam, then leaped from the engine, allowing the train to go off on its own. It crashed into another train at the station, blocking the line for days.

The "Phantom Train" operation became standard practice for the Stockbroker group, and the idea was eventually adopted by guerrilla units elsewhere in France.

By the time late in 1944 when the first Allied troops reached the area in which Stockbroker was operating, Floege was in command of 3,200 men and women. They harassed the German Army constantly. Stragglers and small patrols were killed or captured. Hundreds of soldiers surrendered to members of Stockbroker.

D-Day—June 6, 1944—was a turning point for secret agents in Europe. After D-Day, most of the agents who parachuted into France wore military uniforms. No longer were they dropped in civilian clothes with forged documents. D-Day ended the wartime era of the impostor.

Chapter 12

The Man of a Hundred Lies

Stanley Clifford Weymann lived a full life. He served as a naval representative to the Serbian Embassy and later was a diplomatic agent for the country of Morocco. He was consul-general for Romania and the Peruvian ambassador to the United States.

He was a lawyer. He was a doctor, an adviser to Dr. Loren Adolf Lorenz of Vienna, one of the most famous surgeons in the world during the 1920s. He was an Air Force officer and a naval officer.

When movie superstar Rudolph Valentino died, Weyman took an active part in planning the funeral arrangements, having become the doctor treating Valentino's close friend, Pola Negri.

In 1921, when Princess Fatima of Afghanistan visited the White House and was introduced to President Warren G. Harding, it was Weymann who performed the introduction. At various other times, Stanley Weymann was known as an expert on prison reform and a United Nations reporter.

Weymann's remarkable record had only one flaw. Each of the posts he held was self-appointed. Stanley Clifford Weymann was one of the most creative impostors that ever lived. The State Department, the FBI, and the New York City Police Department knew him well, but by his real name, Stephen Weinberg.

Weinberg did not have the confident and authoritative air that usually goes with being an impostor. He was a quiet, soft-spoken little man, who, when not impersonating military officers, dressed plainly.

Throughout his long career, Weinberg was much more interested in rubbing elbows with the famous and socially important people of the day than he was in swindling anyone. He preferred collecting honors and degrees, however phony they might be, than to building a big bank account.

Weinberg was born in Brooklyn and attended local schools. A year or so after he graduated from high school, he began displaying a college degree from the University of Political Tactics of Charleston, South Carolina. As far as anyone has been able to establish, that institution never existed.

The first roles that Weinberg played as an impostor were those of diplomatic figures. When he was twenty-one, and working in a Brooklyn office, he would sometimes spend his evenings running up big bills at fancy Manhattan restaurants, while announcing to one and all that he was an official representative to the United States from the Country of Morocco. He showed documents to prove it. He made the mistake of stealing an expensive camera during this period, and for that was sent to the state reformatory in Elmira.

Once he was released, Weinberg began disguising himself as an American naval officer, changing his name to Weymann. Lieutenant Commander Stanley Weymann he became. His ruse was quickly discovered and he was sent back to the reformatory.

But Weinberg learned from these experiences. When he was paroled, he planned hoaxes that were much more elaborate.

He telephoned the office of the U.S. Navy in New York, proclaiming himself to be Stanley Weymann, the consul-general from Romania. He said that the Queen of Romania had instructed him to make a diplomatic call upon the battleship *Wyoming*, which was anchored in New York harbor. Taken by surprise, the naval official agreed to allow Weymann to make the visit. A motor launch was assigned to pick him up.

On the day of the visit, Weymann donned an elegant light blue uniform with gold braid at the shoulders. Sailors manning the launch saluted him smartly as he boarded the craft. When the launch approached the *Wyoming*, Weymann looked up to see that the vessel was flying the Romanian flag alongside the Stars and Stripes. A pleased grin crossed his face.

Once aboard the *Wyoming*, Weymann reviewed an honor guard and was taken on an inspection tour of the ship. Afterward, he was invited to dine with the officers in their wardroom.

Before leaving the vessel, Weymann told the officers he would like to return their hospitality by entertaining them at the Hotel Astor in New

York. He booked a private dining room at the hotel in the name of the Romanian consul-general, and made arrangements for a lavish meal.

Hotel officials were impressed. They began to notify local newspapers of the event.

A New York police detective happened to read the story. When he saw the name Stanley Weymann, he knew at once that something crooked was afoot.

On the night of the dinner, Weymann was arrested. The officers he was entertaining were shocked. The captain of the ship shook his head in disbelief. "All I can say," he told reporters, "is that guy sure knows how to put on a hell of a show."

Weinberg pulled off what was perhaps his greatest stunt in 1921. He read that Princess Fatima of Afghanistan was visiting the United States and staying at the Hotel Waldorf-Astoria in New York. The Princess was a striking and unusual figure. She clothed herself in long and colorful Afghan robes, always wore a large jewel in her nose and, on her right hand, a 42-carat diamond, known as "The River of Glory." The Princess was making a personal visit to the United States, not an official one.

As Lieutenant-Commander Weymann, Stanley called on the Princess's hotel suite. He told her that besides being a naval officer, he also represented the State Department, and that he had been asked to escort her to Washington where President Harding was eager to receive her.

The Princess was happy to receive the news. But her joy was diminished when Weymann explained to her that it was an American custom to present gifts to the junior diplomats who arranged such visits. And these gifts, he explained further, consisted of cash. He told the Princess that he thought ten thousand dollars would be sufficient. The Princess turned over that amount to him.

The hoax was now half completed. Weymann then assumed the role of Under Secretary of State Clifford Weymann, and called the White House. He explained to a member of the President's staff that Princess Fatima of Afghanistan was coming to Washington and was anxious to meet the President. When the Princess's wish was relayed to President Harding, he agreed to see her.

As soon as he put down the telephone, Stanley became Lieutenant Commander Weymann again. He accompanied the Princess to Washington, took her to the White House, and introduced her to the President. The three of them chatted briefly.

An official White House photographer recorded the event. His photo depicts the Princess dressed in billowing white robes; her three sons, all dressed formally; the President, looking as if he would rather be someplace else; and Lieutenant Commander Weymann, the former Brooklyn file clerk, standing proudly, garbed in starched Navy whites.

Weymann collected more money from the Princess to pay the hotel bill in Washington. Then he vanished. The hotel never got paid.

In the years that followed, Stephen Weinberg became *Dr.* Stanley Weymann, and landed a position as medical consultant with an American construction company in Peru. He became interested in the legal profession. Twice he would be jailed for impersonating lawyers.

Weinberg even tried his hand at politics. During an election for mayor in New York City, he became a fixture at the Democratic campaign headquarters and was given his own desk.

He impressed everyone as one of the hardest working of all the volunteers. Each morning, it was Weinberg who would be the first to arrive. He immediately began going through the day's mail, which contained campaign contributions. When one of his fellow workers became suspicious that some of the contributions might be ending up in his pocket, Weinberg's political career came to an abrupt end.

Weinberg dropped out of sight, but only for a few weeks. When he emerged again, he was Dr. Clifford Weymann. He managed to get himself appointed as a secretary to Dr. Adolph Lorenz, the famous "bloodless surgeon" of Vienna who was opening a clinic in New York.

He didn't hold his new post very long. It was found that Dr. Weymann was asking for and pocketing fees for patients before allowing them to see the great doctor.

When the story of his hoax appeared in the newspapers, one of Princess Fatima's sons recognized Dr. Weymann as Lieutenant Commander Weymann, the diplomatic representative who had disappeared, leaving behind a mass of unpaid bills. Weinberg was arrested for impersonating a naval officer and sent to prison for two years.

Weinberg was in the limelight again in 1926. When a newspaper reported that actress Pola Negrì had collapsed with grief over the death of the fabled actor Rudolph Valentino, the ever helpful Dr. Weymann called upon her at the hotel, introducing himself as an old friend of Valentino's. He was taken on as Negri's physician and helped her in making the funeral arrangements for Valentino. On the day of the funeral, it was Dr. Weymann's rented limousine that led the procession.

During World War II, Weinberg set up shop as a "Selective Service Consultant," advising young men how to dodge the draft. For a fee of from two hundred to two thousand dollars, he would instruct a draftee how to fake deafness, simplemindedness, or some other ailment.

When the federal government got wind of the scheme, the FBI was assigned to the case. As they closed in on him, they found Weinberg's apartment contained a tremendous array of shoes, hats, jackets, and other clothing which he used in performing his various roles.

Weinberg should have used one of his disguises to make a getaway. The FBI arrested him for operating a draft-dodging clinic, and he was sent to jail for seven years. With time off for good behavior, Weinberg was released in 1948.

Some months after his release, Stanley Clifford Weymann called upon Robert Erwin, head of the Erwin News Service, an agency that provided news coverage for small-town newspapers and radio stations. Weymann asked for a job covering the United Nations. He claimed to be a former newspaperman.

Erwin hired Weinberg on a part-time basis. Weinberg made up for whatever failings he may have had as a writer by displaying a keen sense of what made news and his ability to get interviews with the leading diplomats of the day. "He knew everybody," Erwin once said of him. It wasn't long before Weymann was taken on as a full-time employee.

Weymann became a well-known ond very popular figure at the United Nations Building in New York. Thailand's ambassador to the United States offered him a job as press officer for the Thai delegation. If Weymann were to accept the job, it would mean that he would be a *real* diplomat for the first time in his life.

On the brink of success, Weymann made a rare mistake. He wrote to the State Department in Washington to ask whether his U.S. citizenship would be affected if he accepted the job with the government of Thailand. A State Department officer, who knew of Weymann and his shady career, happened to see the letter.

The ambassador to Thailand was called immediately. The job offer was withdrawn.

And when the Erwin News Service learned the truth about Weymann, they promptly fired him. His fellow employees were sorry to see him go. They admired him for his diligence and intelligence.

In the years that followed, Weinberg drifted from one job to another. He died in 1960, the victim of a crime. He was working as the manager of a motel in Yonkers, just north of New York City. One night, a gunman appeared to rob the motel safe. Little Stephen Weinberg defied him. The gunman shot Stephen dead.